SPLASH

SPLASH

A novel by Ian Don
based on a screenplay by
Lowell Ganz and Babaloo Mandel
and Bruce Jay Friedman
Screen story by Bruce Jay Friedman

A STAR BOOK
published by
the Paperback Division of
W.H. ALLEN & Co. PLC

A Star Book
Published in 1984
by the Paperback Division of
W.H. Allen & Co. PLC
44 Hill Street, London W1X 8LB

Printed and bound in Great Britain by
Anchor Brendon Ltd, Tiptree, Essex

ISBN 0 352 315946

1

Allen Bauer gazed into the sparkling water from the rail of the river cruiser, longing to trail his small hands in its flashing, seductive surfaces. Although he hadn't yet learned to swim, the water looked so inviting as they chugged slowly along the Cape Cod shoreline, past the scattered holiday homes half-hidden among the lush vegetation fringing the little crescent-shaped beaches. Behind him, under a faded awning on the upper deck, a couple of dozen trippers were dancing to the sound of a bored pop group playing a succession of monotonous numbers. 'Watch it now... Watch it now...' droned the lead guitarist-cum-vocalist staring woodenly at his microphone. Allen's fat elder brother Freddie wandered mischievously round the upper deck, draining the odd abandoned cocktail glass with expert dexterity and keeping out of his parents' way. Every few minutes Freddie crept up behind a pretty girl, took out a handful of nickels, dropped them onto the deck and then knelt down on his bare chubby knees to take a good long look up the girl's short skirt. 'Here it comes . . . Here it comes . . .' shouted the singer, idly swigging his rum and Coke between phrases, 'Watch it now...'

'I'm watchin',' Freddie murmured fervently, mesmerised by a pair of frilly scarlet knickers and snatching up his coins just in time to avoid having his ear clipped by a passing steward.

Allen heard the song as if in a dream, watching his own private pictures in the water in a world of his own. The hard wooden rail hurt his bony elbows, but he was aware only of the water gleaming in the sunlight. It frightened him and yet he loved it too. The boiling wash of the boat made it seem almost alive to him and he closed his big dark eyes and listened to its chatter. 'Here it comes . . . Watch it now . . .' it told him as the warm breeze ruffled his dark curly hair and the boat moved gently up and down on the swell.

Freddie had found more treasure near the bar. He scattered his nickels, like a croupier dealing cards, behind three giggling girls at the rail. But no sooner did he get into position than a skinny hand seized his ear and yanked him to his feet.

'Freddie!' yelled Mrs Bauer, a neat woman in very ordinary clothes with a careworn face and dulled eyes, holding onto her hat with her free hand.

Freddie grinned innocently at his mother. 'Gee, I just dropped something, Ma.'

'Ralph, talk to him,' Mrs Bauer pleaded as her burly husband wandered over, and they walked their smirking son out of temptation's way.

Ralph Bauer, relaxed in open shirt and trousers held up with wide braces, and a hat on the back of his head, took a hand out of a pocket and slapped Freddie's head gently.

Mary Bauer dragged Freddie across to the rail on the other side of the deck. 'So listen to your father. Come on over here. We can see Cape Cod,' she cried, shielding her grey eyes.

Ralph Bauer shook his head half-heartedly. 'We were just on Cape Cod . . .' he mumbled and shuffled off towards the bar, hands in pockets again.

Mrs Bauer looked around the deck for Allen. She saw him doubled over the rail staring fixedly into the wake. 'Allen, sweetheart, do ya want to see Cape Cod?' she called, holding Freddie firmly with her other hand.

Allen shook his head without looking round.

'All right, darling. You know where we are if you do,' she waved, steering Freddie towards the bar after her husband.

The crude music jangled in Allen's mind and suddenly he wanted to just blot it all out. 'Here it comes . . .' he whispered, climbing onto the rail as if in a trance. Throwing up his slender arms he jumped and vanished into the lovely silence of the welcoming water.

Somebody screamed. Then more and more people shouted and crowded to the rails and clustered at the windows of the lower deck. Bells rang. A whistle blew. At the stern, the water churned furiously as the propeller reversed. Several lifebelts hit the water. With a gasp of wordless horror, Mary Bauer turned, grabbed her husband and dragged him out on deck. Oblivious of the fuss, Freddie was once more on his hands and knees among the nickels on the bar floor, staring upwards wide-eyed.

Allen too gazed upward at the sunlit surface, his hair rising from his scalp like weed, his smiling mouth open in wonder as he sank to the bottom, waving in the clear water. But then he breathed in and panic hit him. He started flailing desperately towards the light. Something took his hand. A smaller hand clasped his and the panic vanished. Allen looked into the smiling face of a girl, young like himself, with lagoon blue eyes and sinuous blond hair trailing behind her. He felt himself being lured away and he gave himself up to the feeling with joy as the girl drew him gently along beside her through the pearly water.

On the boat the band had stopped playing. Ralph and Mary Bauer stood hunched by the rail, screaming Allen's name over and over again. A sailor dived off the foredeck. Freddie knelt, rapt in mysteries.

Suddenly Allen felt afraid. The girl unclasped her hand and turned sharply away from him, her face twisted with anxiety. Immediately Allen began to sink again, gulping water. The girl disappeared as he lashed his arms and legs helplessly, crying dumbly for help.

Then a powerful arm embraced him. He was pulled strongly upwards and seconds later hands were carrying him aboard, faces pressing close and voices shouting with relief.

'Hey, a towel. Somebody gimme a towel...' his father bellowed.

'Why'd you do that Allen?' Mary Bauer sobbed, dabbing his hair and cradling his head. 'Why'd you do that...?'

*

Allen let them dry his hair and dab at his sodden clothes. He just sat by the rail, gazing steadfastly at the placid water as the boat got under way again and the group clattered into a rock number under its awning. Far out in the bay, he saw the little golden head break surface for a moment as if in farewell. A desolate sense of loss and of longing gnawed away inside him as he watched the strange girl dive out of sight. Then the towel slipped down and covered his eyes.

Unseen by anyone, the girl reappeared and then dived again. No sooner had her head vanished, than a pinkish fin glinting with iridescent scales flicked briefly out of the water in a bouquet of silver spray.

Then it too vanished...

2

It was the peak of early morning business in the wholesale fresh-produce market along the wharves of New York's East River. In the distance across the Brooklyn Bridge, Manhattan's glass and steel skyline shimmered like a promised land, but here paper and plastic garbage blew everywhere, workers humped loaded crates and drove fork-lifts like dodgems, people haggled over deals, grabbed a hotdog with one hand and the phone in the other, and lost their tempers over bruised peaches and fermenting grapes. And everywhere among the open-fronted two-storey warehouse buildings, voices rose in a continuous Babel of warnings, threats and complaints.

'Hey Bauer, where are my goddam cherries?'

In front of RALPH BAUER & SONS: TOP QUALITY PRODUCE – FRESH DAILY a large rangy man of about fifty, with sparse greying hair and a lined leathery face, was standing, feet wide apart, among the crates, yelling into the busy warehouse. He looked to be at the end of his tether and nobody was taking any notice of him.

Eventually Allen Bauer appeared. He was casually but smartly dressed in jeans with a shirt, tie and sports jacket. He had grown into a slim athletic man of twenty-eight, not tall but hard and wiry, with thick dark hair slightly curly, fine eyebrows and a sensuous mouth. His sensitive brown eyes registered trouble as he jogged over to his irate customer armed with a clipboard and ballpoint.

'Sorry Mr McCullough,' he said soothingly, 'they came in

but there was some fog upstate and the Highway Petrol stopped . . .'

McCullough loomed over him like a cliff. 'Where are my cherries, you sonofabitch? If I don't get my cherries in five minutes you don't get your money and you starve and you die . . .' he promised, the sinews in his neck knotting alarmingly.

Allen nodded and grinned unhappily, looking anxiously around the chaotic store. His eye caught a young Puerto Rican with unshaven face and a woolly bobble-hat who was tasting a pineapple. 'Jerry!' he cried, rushing over to him. 'Where the hell are Mr McCullough's cherries?'

Jerry blinked the sharp juice out of his eye. 'They're right here,' he muttered. 'But you gotta take a look at them . . .' he warned.

'Be right back,' Allen waved cheerily, leaving McCullough still yelling for his cherries. 'Show me the worst, Jerry,' he sighed.

Jerry led him across the warehouse to a stack of crates where a scrawny fruit-grower in dungarees and a stained hat was furtively picking out the absolute disasters.

Allen stared at the rotting fruit with a doomed expression. 'Where the hell did you grow these, Augie, under your arms?' he demanded. 'They're just snails with stems. Get'em outta here.'

A telephone bell had been ringing endlessly. Allen walked away to the wall phone with Augie trailing after him. 'Yeah, this is Bauer,' he said, turning his back on Augie's protests. 'Oh hi, honey. What's up?'

'Look we had a lotta rain,' Augie whined. 'So the cherries got a little slime.'

'Hey, honey, I can't hear . . . Can I call you back?' Allen shouted into the phone.

'And you agreed to take'm off my hands.'

Allen swung round indignantly. 'When the hell did I agree to that?'

'Not you. Your brother Freddie,' retorted Augie.

'I can't hear you, Victoria, goddamit,' Allen shouted back

down the phone. 'Yeah, honey... Well this what I'm doing here is important too. I'll call you right back.' He hung up, his eyes blazing. 'So my big brother bought your goddam cherries?'

Augie nodded cunningly. 'Sure. We was playin' poker. He had two pair and I had a flush, but Freddie didn't have no money, so we worked this out see?'

Before Allen could vent his frustration, a sudden shrill screech of tyres, followed by the sound of splintering wood, sent him running out to the front, just in time to see Freddie prising his enormous frame out of the driving seat of a smart red Porsche whose front end was completely buried in cabbages and shattered crates.

'Who put this goddamned fruit here?' demanded Freddie Bauer, shoving his way past the white-faced McCullough, who had narrowly escaped being flattened in the pile-up. 'By the way, I'm just fine if anyone's concerned.' In his vast purple velvet suit, matching cravat, gold-buckled shoes and with his heavily beringed fingers, Freddie couldn't have looked more out of place on the wharf.

'Good morning, Freddie,' Allen called out with icy sarcasm.

His elder brother flung out his huge barrel-like arms in greeting and whooped with triumphant glee. He was clutching two handfuls of magazine copies. 'I made it, baby!' he announced, his jowls quivering with delight and his youthful eyes as bright as diamonds as he waddled into the warehouse. 'I'm in *Penthouse*. They printed my letter!'

Just then McCullough barged his way in front and seized Allen's arm. 'Bauer, I want a simple yes or no,' he muttered through capped teeth.

Allen nodded helplessly. 'Just one more second,' he pleaded, watching Freddie apprehensively.

'I'm in *Forum*... They printed my letter!' Freddie chanted, waving the magazines as he bulldozed among the workers. 'The story's entitled "A Lesbian No More" and they printed every word I wrote. It's a really beautiful story and I want copies given to everyone,' he cried, thrusting copies into people's hands all around him.

'Hey, well, listen, I'm very happy for you,' Allen told him, pulling himself free from McCullough's tenacious grip and attempting a smile.

Freddie embraced Augie enthusiastically. 'Great game the other night. We'll do it again sometime!' he exclaimed. 'Hey listen, everyone. This guy is a great poker player. He cheats like a son of a bitch!'

Allen glanced sidelong at the stack of cherries. 'He sure does,' he laughed drily, grabbing Freddie's sleeve and trying to steer him towards the stairs leading up to the office. 'Listen, Freddie, you and me have to talk,' he said firmly.

Freddie suddenly looked scared, grimacing melodramatically. 'Is it about the petty cash? It was the cleaning girl,' he protested.

'I don't care about the petty cash, Freddie.'

'You don't?' Freddie grinned childishly. 'Well, okay then, it was me. I admit the whole thing.'

Allen shook his head impatiently. 'I still don't care about it Freddie.'

McCullough looked on, stoking up with outraged frustration as Freddie cuddled his younger brother affectionately.

'I just love this guy . . .' Freddie yelled to the whole wharf. 'D'ya hear me? I love him. Give me a kiss,' he murmured, pouting his big lips suggestively. 'Come on, give your big brother a kiss.'

Nervous about McCullough rather than embarrassed by Freddie, Allen backed off, shaking his head vehemently.

Swinging his arm, Freddie seized Allen in a playful headlock. 'What's up, baby. You too big?' he laughed, kissing Allen's hair. 'Hey folks, I just love this guy's head . . .' he grinned.

McCullough finally lumbered over to them.

Reaching into his jacket, Freddie took out a thick wad of notes and stuffed them into McCullough's shirt pocket. 'Hey curly, go wash my car . . .' he scoffed contemptuously.

McCullough flung the money back. 'Where are my

cherries?' he whispered hoarsely.

Shaking free from Freddie, Allen laughed hesitantly and pointed to the nearby crates. 'Yes, Mr McCullough, your cherries are right here. But believe me when I tell you that you are not going to be happy with what we've got for you today . . .'

McCullough gaped at the pulpy fruit with glazed eyes. Then he turned malevolently on Allen. 'And you believe me, Bauer, when I tell you that you are ruined,' he snarled. 'Everyone's gonna hear how you left me high and dry. You're a ghost in this city!'

Allen swallowed hard, racking his brains for a let-out. 'Hey, how would you like some bananas?' he grinned suddenly. 'At cost.'

McCullough flung out a hairy paw. 'Deal,' he snapped.

With a sigh of relief Allen called Jerry over. 'Set up our good friend Mr McCullough. Bananas at cost,' he ordered. Then he hurried away towards the office stairs.

But Jerry came running anxiously after him. 'Allen, here, wait a minute,' he protested. 'I gotta get outta here early today. Remember?'

Allen shut his eyes and slapped himself on the forehead. 'Gee, that's right, Jerry. Today's your big day,' he murmured warmly, thumping the boy encouragingly on the chest.

'Sure is,' Jerry grinned wryly. 'Now don't forget, Allen, ushers have to be there early.'

Allen smiled. 'I'll be there yesterday,' he promised.

Freddie was right behind Allen as he stopped in the outer office at the top of the stairs to ask Mrs Stimler, the secretary, if there were any messages. Mrs Stimler was a vague, grey-haired widow with upswept bifocal spectacles, dressed in a hideous non-matching twinset. Instead of pearls, she wore a key on a string round her neck. Her hair was encased in a mottled plastic bath-cap. Her silent typewriter was covered in dust and her chaotic desk cluttered with bric-à-brac. She gazed at the brothers with kindly recognition as she carried on cutting out recipes from a woman's magazine.

'Yes, your father called. He wants you to call him back,' she reported in a high swooping voice.

Allen and Freddie exchanged raised eyebrows and shook their heads hopelessly.

'Ah, Mrs Stimler, our father passed away about five years ago,' Allen reminded her gently.

Mrs Stimler put down her scissors. 'Right. Should I get him for you, Mr Allen?'

Allen clutched his head with long, sensitive fingers and blinked with the effort of keeping calm. 'No, no, no. I'll deal with it,' he replied. 'You just... you just get on with your work.'

Demurely Mrs Stimler picked up her scissors again and resumed her task.

The two brothers went on through into the inner office. It was peaceful, in semi-darkness, with a couple of shaded lamps and the early sun slanting through half-open venetian blinds. In a corner, an illuminated aquarium bubbled away quietly, its brightly coloured inhabitants swimming endlessly to and fro in serene contentment.

Allen glanced affectionately over at the fish and then threw himself thankfully into the reclining swivel-chair by his desk.

Freddie tapped his forehead. 'What's with Mrs Stimler?' he asked.

'Oh, she had a little accident over the weekend. Got hit in the head by some lightning.'

Freddie's huge body shook with stifled laughter.

'Hey, Freddie, that's not funny,' Allen frowned.

'I'm sorry, Allen. That's not funny.'

Allen shrugged indulgently. 'Besides, she's OK. She can still do things around the office,' he claimed defensively.

Freddie flopped into a chair. 'Like what? Jump-start a truck?' he suggested, guffawing mightily.

Allen got up and went over to feed the fish. He scattered the grains of food with a graceful, almost religious gesture and silently watched the fish popping up to the surface time after time. He stroked the glass tank lovingly with the back of his hand.

'Jump-start a truck . . . !' Freddie repeated helplessly.

Allen walked across to him. 'Freddie, what the hell are you doing down here today?' he demanded disapprovingly.

Freddie shot him a sly sideways glance and paused for effect. 'Maybe I went to the club last night . . .' he hinted.

'So what's new?'

'And maybe I met Mr Buyrite of Buyrite Supermarkets . . . And maybe we had a few drinks . . .' Freddie leered suggestively.

Allen stared at him, uncertain what was coming next.

'And maybe . . . just maybe, we're his new produce-suppliers,' Freddie concluded, examining his fingernails casually.

Allen wandered away and sank into his chair. 'Freddie, I'm real proud of you,' he said with emphatic sarcasm. 'That's really great. Which store?'

Freddie took out a large cigar. 'Not which store. The whole goddam chain!' he announced, lighting up and puffing away smugly.

Allen gripped the edge of his desk tightly. 'I hope you're joking with me right now,' he murmured weakly, tense with foreboding.

Freddie waved his cigar. 'Think big. Be big, my friend.'

Allen gritted his teeth and stared at his brother in silence.

'He was a Green Beret colonel,' Freddie elaborated grandly. 'So I made up a little story about you bein' wounded in 'Nam and now he wants to do business.'

Allen sat tight-lipped and ashen-faced.

Freddie puffed away imperiously. 'The guy's comin' round here this morning to check out the operation.'

Slowly Allen rose to his feet. 'This morning?' he echoed incredulously. 'Oh that's just great, Freddie. This is only chaos down here today. Augie only brings me slimy cherries from upstate . . .'

'So what, brother?'

'Jerry's only getting married this evening. Did you realise that?'

'So what, baby?' Freddie persisted, standing up resentfully. 'I was only out drinkin' with the Buyrite guy all night long...'

'I have to pick up a tuxedo this afternoon...'

'And here I am bustin' my buns...'

'All the way to Forty-Seventh Street...'

'Goddammit, this is a big deal!' Freddie yelled, beside himself. 'Come on, Allen, you can handle it.'

'For crying out loud!' Allen screamed, slumping back into his chair and punching the desk-top. 'Oh sure, I'll handle it...'

Freddie glanced down at the desk critically. 'You should clear up your desk. It always looks like a pigsty in here,' he advised.

'No problem, Freddie. Don't touch the desk.'

'Do what I do,' Freddie insisted, rummaging among Allen's papers, 'and throw it all in a drawer.'

'Don't touch, I have a system on the desk,' Allen hissed, at the end of his patience.

The phone buzzed. There was a tense pause. Then Freddie snatched it up. 'Phone for you,' he grinned helpfully.

With a murderous look, Allen took the phone. Immediately his face froze with guilt. 'Oh, hi there, Victoria. I'm real sorry, honey. No, I meant to call you right back... Hey what's the matter? Your voice sounds kinda funny?'

Freddie had carefully picked up the extension and was sitting eavesdropping on the conversation.

'What? You're moving out?' Allen exclaimed, biting his nails with anxiety. 'Out of the apartment, now, while we're talking on the phone?' He ruffled his hair helplessly. 'OK, I know we were gonna talk about it. But Victoria, don't you think it is just a little impulsive?' he pleaded desperately. 'Hey honey, if we were married you wouldn't just move out like this would you?'

Freddie listened. 'Yeah, she might do just that,' he chuckled.

Allen threw him a blistering look. 'Will you get off the

phone?' he snapped.

Freddie hung up, mumbling an exaggerated apology.

'No, no, no, no, not *you*, Victoria,' Allen tried to explain. 'I was just telling . . . Hey listen, what am I gonna say to . . .?'

'Why don't you tell a guy you're on the phone?' Freddie complained with cruel irony. Shrugging, he stubbed out his cigar and waddled out of the office.

Allen listened for a long time in silence, wiping tears of shock and humiliation from his eyes while Victoria made her speech of final rejection. 'But Victoria, what do you mean, do I love you?' he butted in eventually. 'Well, we met . . . and I . . . well, you moved in, didn't you? No, it's just that it's a very difficult and complicated thing to know . . . Hey, do you love me . . .?' he enquired plaintively.

After a long pause Allen took the receiver from his ear and stared at it, on the verge of sobbing his heart out. 'Well, there you go,' he shrugged, dropping it onto its buttons. He thrust his hands into his pockets and gazed at the aquarium, where the fish sported, brightly oblivious of his misery.

'And there she went.'

He stood there motionless for some time, watching the brilliantly coloured creatures effortlessly twisting and gliding in their endless sunlit dance. Then something jogged in his memory. He tried to concentrate and to bring it to the front of his mind. But it would not come. Like a word on the tip of the tongue, it lingered tantalisingly just out of reach.

3

In its tiny tree-filled churchyard, the church provided an oasis of peace and greenness amid the downtown canyons of concrete and glass. The joyful pealing of bells and the glory of the late sun reflected off the tall office buildings all around and the scent of hundreds of flowers rose like a blessing into the evening sky.

Resplendent in grey tailcoat, stiff shirt, wing collar and striped tie, Allen stood happily at his post in the porch as senior usher, directing the multitude of guests to their seats. 'Hi there. Anywhere but the first three rows, please . . .' he repeated, light-hearted and smiling again after the traumas of Victoria's devastating phone call and the problems at the market earlier in the day.

But his happiness was short-lived. The clink of nickels on the gravel outside alerted him to the arrival of Freddie. He ventured warily outside to find his brother, clad in lemon-coloured topper and tails with gigantic carnation buttonhole, kneeling unashamedly behind a cluster of young ladies in brilliant dresses and full bloom.

'Get up, for chrissake,' Allen hissed, smiling unconcernedly at the milling guests as he tried to haul Freddie to his feet. 'This was embarrassing when you were ten years old. Now it's . . .'

'Listen,' Freddie muttered tipsily, following unsteadily as Allen guided him towards the porch, 'if something works for me, then I stick with it . . .'

Allen kept silent and composed himself as best he could as he resumed his formal duties at the door.

'So Victoria left, huh?' Freddie mused, ogling the flirtatious young beauties from afar.

'By the time I came home she'd already gone,' Allen confirmed, nodding and smiling at an elderly couple who presented their invitation for inspection. 'You know why she left me, Freddie? Because I didn't love her.'

'That bitch,' Freddie spat contemptuously.

The elderly woman turned and glared.

Freddie bowed and grinned amiably. 'She just had puppies . . .' he explained, conjuring the excuse out of thin air.

'Anywhere in the second or third row please,' Allen directed, with exaggerated politeness, shooting a withering glance at his rosy-cheeked brother.

Freddie turned to Allen, unaware of the look. 'Allen, I gotta get more involved in the business,' he confided earnestly, 'and I intend to. I really mean it this time. I mean, I know the business. I was there with Dad at the beginning, remember?'

Allen nodded, praying that he'd be spared any further embarrassment.

Freddie clutched his lapels fervently. 'I just . . . I just need to know. Do we sell fruit and vegetables, or is it just fruit?'

Before Allen could bring himself to reply, Freddie got distracted by a girl in a very low-cut dress. 'Hey there!' he greeted her, winking.

'Hi there,' said the girl. 'Hey Allen, where's Victoria?'

Allen grinned bravely. 'Oh, she's just sick and she couldn't make it today,' he lied.

'Oh that's too bad.'

'Anywhere but the first three rows, Cindy.'

Allen turned back to Freddie. 'Why didn't I love Victoria?' he demanded aggressively. 'Can you answer me that? I mean she had everything. She was bright, she was sensitive, she was beautiful . . .'

'Hey Allen!'

'Oh, hi there. Anywhere but the first . . .'

'Where's our lovely Victoria today?'

'The flu. Yeah, the bad flu. She's awful sick and she's not here.'

'Give her our love will you?'

Allen raised his hands in an embracing gesture. 'Oh sure.' He hugged his chest convulsively. 'I can't even give her *my* love, Freddie. Something in here just is not working . . .' Allen whimpered wretchedly, turning his face into Freddie's ample bosom.

Freddie ruffled his brother's hair sympathetically. 'There are worse organs not to be working, my son,' he pointed out dolefully.

At that moment, a sharp postgraduate-type breezed up wearing a fraternity tie, with a dumb-looking girl on his arm. 'Hey, Allen, where's that gorgeous lady of yours?' he roared heartily.

Allen swung round sharply. 'She's not coming today, OK?' he shouted. 'You want your money back?'

Heads started to turn in the pews nearest the door.

'Hey Allen, I'm real sorry to hear . . .'

'She left me,' Allen blasted on recklessly. 'She moved out and now my life's a shambles. OK, that's the news. You want the weather?' he yelled. 'Anywhere but the first three rows!'

More heads had turned and people were stirring uncomfortably further up the nave. Allen stood with head bowed, breathing hard, his fists clenched tight, struggling to regain his composure.

Freddie put an enormous arm round his trembling brother and shook him gently. 'Hey, you really should lighten up on that guy,' he murmured. 'That's the bride's brother.'

Inside, the organ had started to play with strident urgency.

4

In the dim reddish lighting of the club reception-rooms the wedding guests were mostly all past dancing and they were now lounging around in the plushy upholstered shadows, drinking, giggling, kissing with various degrees of intimacy, and some were sitting together or alone simply staring into the lemon peel and ice cubes. Only one guest was lying across the bar cluttered with dirty glasses, face down in a bowl of pretzels, one hand clutching an empty glass. It was Allen. Beside him, a dishevelled and maudlin Freddie was philosophising in a morose monotone.

'Ya see, drinkin's really a question of algebraic ratios,' Freddie declared, reaching for his Screwdriver. 'How drunk you get depends on how much alcohol you consume in relation to your bodyweight.' He took a huge gulp and considered his popping waistcoat buttons. 'See my point, Allen? It's not that you had a lot to drink... it's just that you're too skinny...'

He lifted his brother back onto his stool. Allen blinked at him unseeingly, his face mottled with sticky pretzels and uttered a long and profound moan.

Freddie sighed and waved to the immaculately red-jacketed bartender near by. 'Hey, Marceau. A bunch more drinks here, please.'

Allen finally opened his eyes and belched an almost melodic protest. 'No, no, Freddie... I don't wanna get drunk,' he groaned through the clustered pretzels, listing precariously on the tall stool.

Freddie grinned solicitously. 'But you *are* drunk, Allen. A sober person would've *reached* for the pretzels.'

Marceau set down two very large drinks. 'Is he gonna be there long?' he enquired wearily, as the band wailed some blues from the almost deserted dance-floor and Allen slumped forward again.

'I don't know,' Freddie smiled.

'Oh, I'm on the bar . . .' Allen mumbled, blowing the tacky pretzels off his lips, 'and somebody's on my mouth.'

'You should be so lucky,' Freddie told him, lifting him off the bar and standing him upright. 'And this stool's in your way. Let me move that for you . . .'

He moved the stool and Allen immediately crumpled to the floor. 'Oh dear, you fell,' Freddie taunted, taking another gulp of his drink.

Allen started to drag himself to his feet and banged his head hard on the overhang of the bar.

'You just love that bar,' Freddie chuckled, taking Allen's head in his hands and gazing solemnly into his sad, dazed eyes. 'You're not havin' a very good day are you, baby?'

'Wasn't that a beautiful wedding ceremony?' Allen sobbed, clutching onto Freddie's mountainous shoulders.

'Oh, that sure was a beautiful ceremony,' Freddie agreed, nodding his small round head and gazing past Allen at a couple of women in slit skirts with deep cleavages who were just wandering past looking rather free and easy.

'It was . . .' Allen insisted, the hot tears welling and blurring Freddie's bulbous Zero Mostel features, 'a lovely . . .'

Suddenly Freddie's face had disappeared. Allen tottered forward as if searching for that rock of stability and sympathy. His knees encountered the back of a low settee and he toppled over it and onto the floor on the other side.

'Gorgeous . . .' agreed Freddie, mincing across to the two girls, pointing his small patent leather boots elegantly. 'Hi there. How are ya doin'?' he asked cheekily, settling himself with some difficulty between them at their table. 'Fabulous Freddie Bauer here.'

'Hi,' they chorused amiably.

*

Allen hauled himself painfully to his feet and eventually wove his way back to the bar, flourishing some orange blossoms he had found under the settee. He sipped his drink noisily and often. After a while he noticed a young couple along the bar, smiling and nodding and glancing at each other more and more frequently. He started moving along the bar in stages towards them, watching them intently as he approached.

'Where did you get those?' the guy was asking, shyly touching the girl's earrings.

'My grandmother's. She gave them to me.'

'She did?' The guy inched closer to her.

'Yes.'

'Oh, they are just beautiful,' said the guy, inching closer still.

Leaning his head on one hand on the bar, Allen waved the blossoms around in the couple's faces. 'You two guys are in love, aren't you?' he mumbled, smiling dreamily.

The young man glanced at Allen's open dress-shirt and untied tie. 'We just met,' he snapped, signalling Allen with his cold blue eyes to beat it.

Allen waved the blossoms again and sipped his drink. 'That does not matter. See, I know about these things,' he persisted in a rambling clogged voice. 'I can see. I can tell. You two guys, you're in love. And I think that's beautiful.'

The man turned to him. 'Thanks,' he said icily and turned back eagerly to the girl. 'I don't live too far from here . . .' he murmured suggestively.

'Do I expect too much out of life?' Allen demanded, gesturing extravagantly with his glass and sending a stream of bourbon and ice cubes into the girl's lap.

'My dress!' the girl gasped. 'I can't believe this!'

Allen dabbed at her breasts with his handkerchief. 'I'm real sorry,' he mumbled, dabbing lower and lower.

'Hey what are ya doin'?' the guy exclaimed, standing up.

'Well, you go ahead and do it. You do it. I don't care . . .' Allen droned on, mopping at the mess on the bar.

The girl jumped up, staring at the vivid rust stain adorning her frock. 'Both of you. You're both creepy,' she gasped, flouncing away, while the guy followed her, desperately trying to make things right again.

The bartender took Allen's empty glass and wiped the bar.

Allen leaned across to him. 'I don't ask that much, do I?' he demanded, patting at his tear-stained cheeks with the wilting orange blossoms. 'I mean I don't ask to be famous or rich, and I don't ask to play centre field for the New York Yankees or anything.'

Marceau deserted him to serve another couple who had just come up to the bar.

'I just want to meet a woman . . .' Allen confided to them along the bar. 'I want to meet a woman and then . . . I want to fall in love and I want to get married and have a kid and . . . I want to see him play a part in the school play. That's not much, is it?' He paused and blinked at the newcomers, waiting for some kind of reaction. But they pretended he wasn't there and gazed fondly into one another's eyes and drank long slow draughts.

'But I'm just kidding myself,' Allen eventually whispered into the orange blossoms. 'It's never going to happen. I'm gonna grow old and I'm gonna grow lonely and I'm gonna die . . . And I'll be surrounded by a bunch of rotten fruit.'

Freddie's thunderclap guffaws stirred him from his miserable reverie. He slid off the stool and wandered across to their table.

'Really? No kiddin'?' Flanked by the laughing lovelies, Freddie was chuckling away, smoking his cigar in short urgent puffs and jangling his bracelets playfully. '*No kidding*?'

'Freddie.'

'Hey, Allen. I want ya to meet some friends of mine . . . This is Connie and this is Jill,' Freddie boomed expansively. He leered up at him. 'Your Connie. Connie Tiger!' he assured him.

Allen nodded curtly, wiping his eyes and sniffing. 'Hi,' he said, with a feeble smile. 'Freddie. Could I talk to you, please?' Allen pleaded quaveringly.

'Oh absolutely. Absolutely,' Freddie agreed, rising.

Allen moved a little way off.

'Sure, sure, sure . . .' giggled the girl.

'I'll be right back, sweethearts, and then we'll whisper some more,' Freddie assured them.

He waddled over to Allen, rubbing his plump hands greedily together. 'Boy, have I got some whispers for you. Oh God, oh God, oh God,' he sang. 'Pack your bags tonight my boy. We're going to Rio.'

In the background the girls sat swaying sensuously to the music from the dance-floor.

'These two have got a time-sharin' condominium in Rio,' Freddie babbled, nudging Allen with his broad hip. 'We're going to share some time with them . . . Oh yes . . . Oh God . . .'

Allen shook his head emphatically. He seemed suddenly a little less drunk and his tears were gone. 'No, Freddie. I'm not going to Rio, I'm going to Cape Cod,' he said, turning and walking away.

Freddie stared after his brother, speechless. Then he scuttled after him. 'What the hell you talking about . . . Cape Cod?' he scoffed, grabbing Allen's sleeve. 'Why would you go to Cape Cod?'

Allen looked even more sober now. His eyes were bright with an idea rather than with tears. 'I don't know, Freddie. Because I like Cape Cod. I feel better up there. Because . . .' Allen hesitated and shook his head very slowly. 'I look at the water and I feel closer to something. I don't know . . .'

Freddie looked dumbfounded. 'Cape Cod over Rio? Are you all right in there?'

Allen nodded calmly.

'Let me drive you.'

'No, Freddie.'

'Let me drive you up there,' Freddie insisted aggressively. 'It's a long drive.'

'No.'

Freddie shrugged and cast his arms around as though he were reaching out for some unanswerable argument. 'You got enough money?'

'Yeah. I got plenty.' Allen grinned.

Freddie leaned closer. 'Can I have some then?' he growled, jerking his head over towards his new acquaintances in the shadows.

Allen smiled and patted him lovingly on both cheeks. Then he wheeled round and ran quickly out of the club.

5

Outside Allen stopped dead as the fresh night-air hit him like a blow from a boxing-glove. He took a few deep breaths and then ran along the crowded Broadway sidewalk in search of a cab, his loose tie and open waistcoat flying and his hired tailcoat flapping off one shoulder. Eventually he spotted an empty cab and he dived across the busy street and thumped on the windows, causing skids and irate blasts on horns all around him. He yanked open the door and threw himself into the back.

The cab started off automatically. 'Where to?' asked the driver disinterestedly after they had gone a hundred yards or so.

'Cape Cod, Massachusetts.'

Allen was thrown violently forward against the glass partition as the cab dug its nose into the ground in an abrupt halt.

'You break that and you pay for it,' the driver threatened.

Allen sat himself up again, his forehead numb and his head splitting. 'Oh, I'm so sorry,' he shouted. 'I usually don't enjoy smashing the glass with my face, ya know.'

The driver looked at his unkempt passenger in the mirror, nodding wearily. 'Okay, Mac. Cape Cod. That's about three hundred miles. You got the cash?' he asked impassively.

Allen rummaged around in the suit pockets and leaned forward holding up a double handful of twenty and fifty-dollar bills like a sacrificial offering. He was instantly hurled back into the seat as the cab leaped forward, wheels spinning, and roared out into the stream of late-night traffic in a wild and reckless U-turn.

'What is this?' Allen yelled as he was thrown sideways. 'The Indianapolis?'

'This is Broadway,' the driver yelled back, 'and we're goin' North.'

Allen lay back and closed his eyes. Soon he was asleep and dreaming. Dreaming of the lazy light on the water and childhood memories of the smell of the sea.

In the cold dawn light, Cape Cod was not quite as Allen had remembered it. A greyish haze covered the sky and a strong onshore breeze was whipping up the water in the bay into jagged froth-tipped waves which roared in up the beach in endless succession. Behind him, the crescent of still-flickering lights around the curve of the bay bore witness to the holiday-home boom of the last twenty years, and a thick forest of bare masts swung and clattered around the extended wooden jetties in the harbour. But he gulped the bracing air bravely and stared across to the flat island in the distance.

Eventually, the early sun bathed the island in a pale rose light as though it were a special place, a sanctuary perhaps. Allen stood motionless in the sand for a long time, just gazing across the foaming bay at the promised land, a faint smile playing over his haggard face. New York and the market and Victoria seemed a lot more than three hundred miles away now and it was blissful.

A little way along the beach he had noticed a forty-foot tugboat tied up at a jetty. Now three men were struggling to unload three or four bulky wooden crates from the back of a pick-up parked on the beach near by. Allen eyed the solid tugboat with approval and then looked back out to the island. It was worth a try. Hands deep in the pockets of the crumpled suit, he wandered casually over to them.

The unloading was being supervised by an academic-looking man aged about thirty-five. He had thick black curly hair, black eyebrows and a black Groucho Marx moustache. A pair of thick black-rimmed spectacles was perched half-way along his enormous nose. He wore a thick woollen polo-neck sweater and jeans tucked into gigantic gumboots.

'Careful with that. Be careful with that!' he shouted at the two young fishermen helping him as they dropped a crate heavily into the sand.

One lad was tall and lanky, the other short and solid. They gazed at their boss with slow pale-blue eyes.

'What do you think you are handling there? This is delicate scientific equipment,' he scolded them. He indicated a THIS WAY UP arrow stencilled on the side of the crate and now pointing into the beach. 'Hold it. You see this? It means this end up,' he explained painstakingly slowly. 'You know what that means? It means this end up. So why don't you try holding that end up?'

The two lads bent willingly to obey the instructions.

But the man waved them away impatiently. 'No, no. Get away. I'll do it myself.' He grappled vainly with the heavy box for several minutes. Then he glared at the watching boys. '*Give me a hand*!' he yelled.

As they all struggled to right the crate, Allen strolled up to them. 'Morning...' he said brightly.

The two lads looked up and nodded. 'Mornin',' they drawled.

Allen turned to their incongruous-looking boss. 'Excuse me, sir, I've been dropped off on the wrong side of the beach and I was wondering if you could take me over to the island?' he ventured politely.

The man glanced at him suspiciously. 'Well, we're not going to... We're taking the boat somewhere else... We're not going out there,' he replied evasively, tugging at the capsized crate furiously.

Allen looked around the deserted beach. 'Well, have ya seen anyone else along the beach here?'

Impatiently the man gestured his lads back to work. 'No. Just myself and the moron twins,' he grunted.

The taller, elder boy straightened up again. 'We're not twins...' he drawled resentfully.

Allen frowned at the assortment of crates still in the pick-up. 'What is all this stuff anyway?' he asked casually.

The man sprang up and glared at him. 'I knew it!' he shouted angrily. 'Who sent you here? Dr Ross from Chicago?'

Allen blinked disconcertedly, his head still very tender from the previous night's events. 'Who's Dr Ross from Chicago?'

Pushing his spectacles back up his nose, the man circled him warily, as if he were examining some dangerous forensic specimen. 'Who is Dr Ross . . . ?' he snorted, smiling sarcastically. 'You're good, you are. I suppose you're just some harmless beachcomber who happens to wear a tuxedo!' he laughed derisively. 'How dare you try to horn in on someone else's research.'

Allen shrugged. 'Look, I'm just a guy tryin' to get out to the . . .'

The man was now crouching in a hostile posture in front of him, almost like a karate expert. 'Walter Kornbluth is not a man to be taken advantage of,' he warned, with a sneer of contempt. 'So you just stay out of my way, sonny.'

He lifted one end of the crate. 'All right let's move,' he commanded.

Shaking his head in bewilderment, Allen looked on while the younger brother took the other end and they heaved the box onto the jetty with a supreme effort and carried it towards the wallowing tugboat.

Meanwhile the elder lad, dressed in an outsize boiler-suit and woollen hat, came up to Allen's shoulder. 'There's a guy down the beach there runs folk out to the island . . .' he confided mournfully, his long face seemingly filled with unspoken troubles.

'What's the name?'

The boy gazed intently into Allen's eyes. 'The guy or the island?'

Allen stared back at Kornbluth who was just stepping precariously onto the tugboat backwards. Then he squinted across at the sunlit island out in the bay. 'Thanks. I'll find him,' he waved and set off towards the marina.

6

Two hours later, Allen was sitting nervously in the bow of a tiny dinghy as it puttered asthmatically across the bay. The wind had dropped, the sun was rapidly getting warmer in the clear sky and the sea had calmed itself to a light, regular swell. It was all much more as he had remembered it. Nevertheless, he clung to the sides of the boat with white-knuckled hands and stared with queasy anxiety at the gigantic figure slumped in the stern clad in sweatshirt, seaman's cap and sawn-off jeans, who was steering the hesitant outboard with a complacent grin over his greasy face.

'What's the matter, son?' the huge man enquired after a while. 'You look a little nervous.'

Allen did his best to smile back, his body tensed like a spring. 'Yeah . . . well . . . truth of the matter is, Fat Jack . . . I never learned to swim,' Allen croaked.

Fat Jack examined him with beady eyes. 'Ya can't swim?' he growled, cradling the tiller under his blubbery arm.

'No sir,' Allen grinned bleakly, wishing the water could be flat as a plate-glass window.

Fat Jack shook his neckless head, gurgling with cynical amusement. Then he started to swing his vast three-hundred-pound frame from side to side, causing the dinghy's gunwales to touch the water at each terrifying dip. 'Then ya wouldn't want me to do this . . .' he grunted sadistically.

Allen clung to the boat like a child to its pram, his mouth gaping in horror and his eyes wide. 'Please, Fat Jack. Please don't. No!' he whimpered, panicking as water started to ship over the sides. 'Look, cut it out, Fat Jack. There's water comin' in the boat!' he screamed.

The gross buffoon stopped rocking the dinghy. 'OK, OK. Just havin' a little fun,' he muttered with a sly wink.

They puttered on for a while longer and Allen began to relax a little, holding his grey face up to the sun and enjoying the warm breeze in his hair. His mouth still felt like a drain, but the sea air was at last beginning to make him feel cleansed and renewed.

Then suddenly the motor hesitated, coughed several times and then died completely.

Immediately Allen became tense and anxious all over again. 'What's wrong, Fat Jack? What's the matter with it?'

Fat Jack shook his head in disgust and pulled the starter cord a few times. But the engine refused to start. 'Guess when I rocked her I got a little water in the engine...' he speculated, picking a hammer out of the bottom of the boat between his filthy feet. 'I can fix it, son. I'm mechanical,' he boasted complacently.

Allen sat rigid in the bow while Fat Jack twisted round and banged the engine cowling a few times with the hammer. Then Jack yanked the starter cord to and fro for a while. Still nothing happened.

'Did you fix it yet?'

Jack shook his bullet head and spat copiously. 'Na, I'll have to go back for the other boat,' he drawled, clambering awkwardly to his feet.

Allen gasped as the dinghy rocked violently. 'You'll what?'

With surprising agility, Fat Jack dived over the side.

Panic-stricken, Allen tried to dodge the sheet of water which sloshed into the tiny craft. 'Where... where are you going?' he yelled.

Fat Jack was already moving easily away with a lazy backstroke. 'Back to the dock,' he shouted. 'I can swim it. It's only a few miles. I'll be back with the little boat...'

Scarcely believing his ears, Allen glanced down at the nine-foot tub pitching and tossing under him. 'This is the *big* boat?' he muttered.

But Fat Jack was out of earshot, heading for the distant harbour.

Much further out in the bay, the tugboat was riding at anchor and Walter Kornbluth – now dressed in diving gear minus helmet – was peering intently through binoculars at the lone figure in the tiny dinghy.

'I knew it! I just knew that guy came here to spy on my activities,' he murmured ominously, his eyes narrowing with outraged hatred. Abruptly he swung round, almost losing his balance on the rolling deck. 'I want to go down. I want to go down right now!' he ordered.

His crew, consisting of the two slow brothers, studied the outlandish figure with sceptical amusement. 'Hey, Mister Cornbeef . . .' drawled the elder.

'Kornbluth,' snapped Walter, snatching up the face mask and related items of equipment.

'Watcha lookin' for down there? Buried treasure?' The brothers shook with silent mirth.

Kornbluth flapped clumsily towards them in the unfamiliar gear. 'You want to know what I am looking for boys? I'll tell you.'

Shoulder to shoulder, the boys shuffled forward eagerly.

Forcing his way between them, Walter shouted into alternate ears. 'It's none of your goddam business. That's what I'm looking for. Now get outta my way!'

Pulling on the helmet and mask, Kornbluth checked out his equipment haphazardly. He slung an enormous, heavy underwater camera round his neck, gave the air line and nylon rope a tug or two and tottered with sagging knees to the side. Diving in a travesty of the belly-flop, he disappeared into the clear water.

The brothers stared lethargically into the depths. Then the elder one pointed to the yellow tube hanging over the side.

'Let's pee down his air hose . . .' he suggested.

Allen had plucked up the courage to crawl gingerly to the stern of the dinghy. He picked up the hammer and beat a frenzied tattoo on the battered cowling surrounding the ancient engine. But it had no effect.

'Shit, shit, shit,' he yelled, scowling at the silent machinery.

He gazed around the bay in desperation. He could see one or two yachts and small boats, but they were all miles away. Gritting his teeth, he slowly stood up. He braced his foot against the stern board and took hold of the handle of the starter cord. Balancing himself as best he could, he gave a mighty tug.

There was an explosive growl and the engine erupted into life, suddenly driving the boat unexpectedly forward. Allen was thrown off balance and the dinghy shot away from under him, hurling him into the water in a graceful arc. He flailed himself back up to the surface and dog-paddled frantically as the boat sped round in a tight curve. It circled him relentlessly as he struggled and screamed for help, swallowing water and tensing up in panic.

As he fought to keep his head above the surface, he suddenly saw the boat coming straight at him only yards away.

'Jesus . . .' he gasped, desperately trying to dive under and out of the way, but he was helpless in the tight tailcoat and boots. He heard the engine vibrating through the water as it drove the boat over him. The keel cracked him sharply on the forehead and he sank like a stone, upside down. Bright lights exploded in his head, but their fantastic strobing quickly faded to a numb and silent blackness as he sank down and down, without consciousness and without memory.

His wallet slipped out of the inner pocket of the coat and opened like the wings of some small, undiscovered sea-creature as it floated gradually to the pearly bottom.

But slim hands gently took hold of Allen's nerveless fingers and without panic drew him quickly but calmly along through the bright water. Long fair tresses brushed his face as the weed parted and the shoals of fish flashed away. Without knowing, Allen followed and his body relaxed and yielded and gave itself up, just as it had done once before.

7

Somebody was hammering on the back of Allen's head. As he rose up through the increasingly intense layers of pain, a series of blurred images flashed blindingly behind his eyes. Freddie raining blows on him with rolled up copies of *Penthouse* ... Mr McCullough beating him over the head with a banana ... Fat Jack smashing his skull with his hammer out in the boat ...

Gradually he realised that it wasn't someone hammering, but the sun beating down on his back. He tried to spit the gritty pretzel crumbs out of his dry mouth. Then he realised that it was grains of sand.

He lay face down in the shallows for a long time, feeling his body washing slowly back to life and listening to the quiet, rapid rush of small waves around his feet. Eventually the banging in his head began to fade to a dull throbbing. With a croak of agony, he dragged himself up onto his knees. Last of all he opened his eyes a fraction. Blinding white sand stunned him, but a sweet warm breeze flooded his nostrils with the scent of grass and flowers. He peered cautiously out at what looked like a world of undulating dunes, green and blooming with brilliant flowers beyond the sand.

For a moment he thought he was dead. Part of him might be in Paradise, but his head was surely in Hell. Then the memory of the day before speedily returned when he glanced down at his sodden dress-clothes. He recognised the feeling of dry tight skin around the eyes as one of the symptoms of the earthly hangover. Purgatory after all, he decided.

Clenching his teeth, he tried to stand up, but his legs

collapsed into a wobbling tangle. Eventually he got back to his knees and was about to try again, when suddenly something moved nearby on the skyline along the top of the dunes. He looked up and saw a stir of grass and leaves. Then he made out a mass of long, blond, crinkly hair. He rubbed his eyes and blinked a lot. Now he could see a face in shadow. Two piercing blue eyes, sculpted cheeks and a wide luxurious mouth.

'Hallo . . .' he groaned, in a cracked, hoarse voice.

The girl did not respond. She just gazed at him.

Allen's head split into an infinity of questions. 'D'you have any idea . . . how I got here . . . ?' he muttered, wincing at the loudness of his own words. 'Did you save me . . . ?'

The girl rose from the grass. Her thick tumbling hair shrouded her breasts and most of her body, but Allen realised that she was naked except for a necklace of some kind. He managed to force himself onto his feet, despite the cruel throbbing behind his eyes. 'Do you speak English?' he shouted, clutching his bursting temples.

The silence of the figure made him think that perhaps after all it was a vision. He took a couple of groggy steps up the beach. Instantly the creature took fright and vanished along the dunes. Then she suddenly reappeared, running down the sand towards the water. When she reached the edge she stopped and turned to him.

Allen smiled. He thought she smiled. Then he thought she was walking towards him, her brown silky body rippling like water. Between her bell-like breasts hung a golden necklace set with turquoise and with pearls. She glided up to him, put her slender arms around him, drew him towards her and kissed him full on the lips with her strong but gentle mouth.

Then she turned and ran lightly into the waves.

For a moment Allen was unable to move. Then he emerged from the trancelike daze and called after her. 'Hey. Come back. Please, just tell me who you are . . .' he stammered, staggering into the shallows.

But the radiant figure plunged into the water and disappeared. Soon she reappeared further out, the sun glinting on her hair and her glossy skin.

Allen stumbled back and forth in the water, waving his arms and calling out to her. 'I can't swim . . . Come back . . .' he pleaded. 'I've got to talk to you. Can I call you? What's your number?'

The creature disappeared again. Allen shaded his hammering eyes and stared at the twinkling water, but it remained unbroken. 'Why the hell didn't I ever learn to swim . . .' he repeated over and over through clenched teeth, ruffling his hair as he turned and waded back to the beach.

Behind him, the girl suddenly arced out of the swell like a dolphin. As her head and shoulders plunged back into the water, a gleaming silvery fin flickered briefly above the surface like a blade, with a glimpse of a rainbow-coloured tail beneath. Then it vanished.

When Allen glanced back at the sea there was nothing. He stood for what seemed hours on the dunes just gazing into the bay. Then all at once the words of a forgotten song came into his mind again: 'Here it comes . . . Watch it now . . .' As the sun waned, the white sand no longer hurt his eyes so badly.

'I just gotta stop drinking . . .' he told himself as he turned and wandered inland, away from the dunes.

Out in the bay, the girl dived deeper and deeper among the weed-clad rocks beneath the spot where Allen had been thrown out of the dinghy. Eventually something caught her eye and she reached into a narrow crevice and retrieved the wallet. It was as if she had known all the time that it was there. She hung motionless among the gently caressing fish and studied its contents with a smile of curiosity. Allen's credit cards were exposed in a transparent sleeve and the girl focused eagerly on the recurring words NEW YORK.

Something seemed to occur to her. She closed up the wallet and swam swiftly deeper and further out into the bay. Shoals of striped fish parted to let her pass and then immediately closed together again as if familiar with her presence. She glided through a gap in the rocks and suddenly froze, quite still but slowly drifting.

At that moment Walter Kornbluth turned and saw her. Through his face mask, his spectacles slid down his nose as he goggled in total disbelief at the apparition floating seventy or eighty feet away from him through the limpid water. For the first few seconds he was struck dumb. Then his mouth moved wildly.

'It's *her*... It's a... It is a *mermaid*...' he yelled, his trapped voice deafening him inside the helmet. He struggled to manipulate the bulky camera he'd been using to photograph a nearby turtle. But just as he focused on the astonishing creature, his foot slipped and he dropped the valuable instrument onto the rocks.

Then the glorious creature flicked her tail and swam powerfully away.

'Wait a minute... Wait a minute...' yelled Walter, his ears numb and his eyes popping like a frog's as he watched the wide, double-crescented fin sweeping up and down at the end of the sinuous tail, driving the iridescent creature quickly out of sight.

Maddened with frustration, he picked up the camera and aimed it uselessly into the empty water, stabbing at the shutter button in a futile frenzy. Then he grabbed his umbilical and started yanking it harder and harder, as if he were trying to commit suicide as a result of his misfortune, all the time screaming into his fogged-up mask a continuous war-cry of vindication: 'I've seen her... I've seen her... She's here... She exists...'

The golden creature glided down among the reefs beyond the mouth of the bay until she came to a deep trench where a vast dark shape loomed against the sunlight above. It was the rotting hull of a wrecked three-master sailing ship, leaning at a sharp angle in its rocky grave, its masts and spars still bearing a few rags of sail and ends of shrouds. She swam through a gaping hole in its high stern and into the chart-room, where rolled maps and sounding charts were still lying in place in their racks.

Taking several maps down from the wall, the creature

unrolled them and spread them out over the crumbling table. For some time she traced the wavering outline of the East Coast United States from north to south and back again. On one of the maps she found the words NEW YORK. Smiling, she compared the words with those on the credit card. Then she closed the wallet and gazed for a long time at the map, as if memorising it.

A turtle swam through the chart-room and she reached out and brushed its shell with her hand as it passed by close to her. Eventually she rolled up the maps and replaced them in their racks. Then she gave a flashing thrust with her tail and shot out through the hole in the stern and disappeared.

8

Late next morning, Allen walked onto the market wharf and threaded his way silently through the maze of crated produce. Normally he relished the smell of the newly arrived oranges and onions and all the other stuff, and he usually kept up a barrage of greetings and repartee with the other dealers and the workers. But today was different. He was late, his head hurt and he felt totally disorientated. The white bandage round his head quickly became a cue for endless jibes and comments which he steadfastly ignored – at least until he reached his office.

'Hi,' cooed Mrs Stimler, glancing up from her crochet. 'You're not early this morning, Mr Bauer. And what happened to your head? Lightning?'

Allen paused to pick up the modest pile of mail from her chaotic desk. 'No, no, no, Mrs Stimler. Just a boat hit me.' He opened his screwed-up eyes a little wider. Mrs Stimler gazed back at him through her bifocals with remote sympathy. She was wearing her Playtex Cross-Your-Heart brassière, size 40C, over the top of her nondescript mottled blouse.

'Ah . . . Mrs Stimler . . .'

'Yes, Mr Allen?'

Allen stared at the snow-white lacy scaffolding splendidly supporting his secretary's considerable bosom for all to admire. He gave up. 'Ah . . . no, it's nothing,' he mumbled.

'So nice to have you back,' she said with a coy smile.

Allen nodded and walked through into his office to begin waging the day's unequal struggle against suppliers like

Augie, partners like Freddie, and customers like Mr McCullough.

Just across the river, on the sloping sunlit grass underneath the optimistic arm of the Statue of Liberty, Stan Zeltonoga, the Chief Tour Guide, resplendent in brown tunic, Sam Brown belt, brown jodhpurs, brown Mountie hat and brown boots, was routinely shepherding the last boatload of sightseers before his lunch break. Behind him, the twin towers of the World Trade Centre and the Manhattan skyline provided a dramatic backdrop for his bland patter.

He cleared his throat and straightened his brown tie, his sallow round face settling itself into a neutral mask of educational zeal: 'Welcome to the Statue of Liberty...' he intoned, gesturing vaguely upwards. '.... The statue was a gift from the French people. It has come to symbolise hope for oppressed peoples everywhere...'

'It's green...' some kid blurted out.

Stan ignored the sacrilege. 'Over the course of a century, Miss Liberty has seen the New York skyline, which once she dwarfed, rise in great mountains of stone and steel...'

'But she's lookin' the wrong way,' another wag observed.

As Stan droned on, the two or three dozen tourists gazed dutifully upwards.

But behind them, a naked, golden-haired girl was climbing out of the water near the boat steps. She crouched below the parapet for a while until the sun had dried her body. Then she vaulted nimbly over the railing and stood at the bottom of the embankment, gazing around her with delighted astonishment. Her hair reached almost to her knees and the wind caused the intricate necklace between her breasts to ring faintly like tiny bells. Her keen eyes took in the surroundings with eager excitement.

Stan ushered his party towards the entrance in the base of the massive plinth under the statue. 'If you'll kindly go inside, Miss Simpkins will continue the tour,' he urged them, his mind more and more preoccupied with visions of pastrami on rye. 'OK, come on, here we go. Don't touch my hat!' he warned some playful kid, in a Bilko voice. 'Don't ever touch my *hat*!'

At that moment a bunch of stragglers came up the grass slope from the landing stage.

Stan checked his tie and reluctantly repeated his introduction: 'Welcome to the Statue of Liberty... The Statue is a gift from the French people. It has come to symbolise hope...'

Something highly irregular had caught Stan's eye down by the water's edge. He pretended not to have seen it. '... Symbolise hope for naked women everywhere... Bocci Balls!' he yelled, pointing at the golden lady from the sea.

The group turned to look. The naked girl was walking slowly up the grass towards them, smiling at everything around her. Cries of shock, delight, outrage, disgust, disbelief, lust and even indifference erupted on all sides. People from the main party deserted Miss Simpkins and came crowding outside to see what was going on.

With the men in advance, most of the visitors ran off down the slope to greet the unscheduled attraction...

'Hey can I take your picture, Miss?'

'Lift ya hair up higher so we can see.'

'My picture. Take my picture!' pleaded a silver-haired man in a check suit, putting his arm round the girl's shoulders and burying his moustache in her ear, as his blue-rinsed wife looked on in horror from the entrance above.

'Was a gift straight from the French people... Hey, come on, you guys!' Stan was shouting hysterically.

By the landing steps another man shoved his wife away from the 25c telescope and swung it right round to focus on the stunning figure as she advanced up the slope like a goddess with her followers.

'Miss Liberty has seen the New York skyline...' Stan battled to retrieve his audience from temptation as they flashed and clicked away with frenzied motorised shutters, cine cameras and videos.

*

Eventually a couple of cops appeared and fought their way through the rapidly swelling crowd. 'Get outta the way. Let's see what's goin' on here,' bellowed a red-faced Irish policeman. He grabbed the naked girl's arm with admirable professional detachment. 'This here ain't California, Miss,' he growled. 'We don't go for this kinda stuff up here.'

The girl stared blankly at him, as if she did not understand a single word.

As the cops led her quickly up to the entrance to the Statue the crowd jeered and tried to follow, but the doors were barred and they hung around restlessly outside.

Half an hour later, they gave their heroine a tumultuous send-off and she waved to them like a Hollywood star as the cops escorted her to a police launch clad in an outsize MISS LIBERTY T-shirt reaching almost to her knees.

During the short crossing over to Manhattan, a long-suffering detective attempted to question the strange young woman.

'She don't speak no English,' the Irish patrolman informed him.

'And you do?'

The patrolman handed over Allen's sodden wallet, shrugging off the insult.

The detective flipped through it cursorily. 'Who is this guy Bauer?'

The patrolman shrugged. 'Perhaps she mugged him.'

'Lucky guy.'

Freddie Bauer was in his element. Dressed in a flashy three-piece suit complete with carnation buttonhole and waving a large cigar he had been showing Mr Buyrite and his associates round the business. Meanwhile Allen had done his best to clear up the office and get some kind of readable financial statement prepared.

Mr Buyrite, a shortish gentleman with a Ronald Colman moustache, rings on every finger and wearing a homburg hat with an overcoat thrown across his shoulders like a cape, seemed reasonably impressed.

After they had toured the warehouse he turned to his ebullient host. 'OK, is that enough or do you want more?' he enquired in a nasal whine.

Freddie held up his hands in ecstatic deference. 'No, that's plenty, Mr Buyrite,' he boomed. 'That's all the business we can handle right now.' He offered to lead the way up to the office. 'Shall we talk terms, gentlemen?' he suggested with a knowing smile.

At that moment, Allen came wandering down the stairs looking pretty fragile. Jerry was at his elbow with some problem or other.

'But I don't have the slightest clue to what's goin' on . . .' Jerry complained, scratching his lank hair through his woollen hat.

'And you haven't been married even forty-eight hours yet,' Allen muttered to himself. He waved his hand in dismissal. 'Don't worry about it Jerry. We'll sort it out first thing in the morning,' he decided wearily.

Mr Buyrite greeted him gravely at the bottom of the stairs.

'Ah, Bauer . . . your brother told us about your unfortunate experience in Viet Nam,' he said solicitously.

The four or five assorted heavies clad in a variety of business attire standing around Buyrite contemplated Allen's bandaged head impassively.

Allen gave Buyrite a puzzled, wide-eyed look. 'What's that?' he replied absently.

Freddie bustled over to Allen and leaned into him with an urgent grimace. 'That incident in Viet Nam . . .' he muttered. 'Remember?'

Allen frowned in confusion at the intimidating semi-circle of prize-fighter faces confronting him.

'That grenade goin' off right in your helmet,' Mr Buyrite added with a bleakly sympathetic smile. 'Does it still bother you Mr Bauer? You're wearing a bandage, after all.'

Allen gave Buyrite a sickly smile. He felt on the brink of screaming, or running amok and punching people. He was saved by Jerry, who was waving the wall phone at him.

'Hey, Al. Call for you.'

He glared at Freddie and grinned charmingly at Buyrite and his henchmen. 'Excuse me, gentlemen, I'll be a moment,' and he went over and took the phone.

Freddie and the others saw Allen's face undergo an amazing transformation as he listened to the caller. The thundercloud expression he had worn all day suddenly disappeared. He smiled, then he laughed and shook his head in happy disbelief. 'OK... OK, I'm on my way...' he shouted excitedly, dropping the receiver so that it was left dangling at the end of the coiled cable.

Allen raced past the astonished Buyrite contingent and the gaping Freddie and jumped into his car parked among the apple crates.

Freddie waddled quickly after him. 'Hey, Allen, where you goin'?' he demanded in consternation. 'What the hell...'

Allen shot forward, just missing a forklift coming into the warehouse and careered away along the wharf, his hand hard on the horn.

Freddie stared open-mouthed after him. Then he hurried back to his prospective customers with a smile of abject apology on his pale perspiring face.

'What happened there?' Buyrite demanded.

Freddie thought quickly. 'Telephone!' he suddenly exclaimed.

'Telephone?'

'Yeah. You see he was on the phone in 'Nam when the grenade exploded and ever since then ... he runs and gets in a car and drives away,' Freddie explained, as if his words were a model of logic.

'Oh,' said Buyrite, glancing round at his expressionless colleagues.

'I don't know why. It just happens.'

'Oh.'

Freddie grinned at them and took a puff at his cigar. It had gone out. 'Let's review this deal, shall we?' he suggested desperately, ushering his visitors upstairs.

9

After a reckless drive across the Brooklyn Bridge and round the top of Manhattan, Allen skidded up outside the police station he had been summoned to and double-parked an empty patrol car. Jumping out, he ripped off his bandage and briefly examined his wound in the wing mirror. Then he flung the bandage into the gutter, dived over the back of the police car and nearly flattened a passer-by on the side-walk as he bounded up the steps and through the doors of the precinct headquarters. Inside, he ran up more stairs and finally erupted into the long, low office.

'Hey, pardon me. Excuse me. Hey, officer, sir . . .' Allen shouted, leaning over the counter and dancing impatiently from foot to foot.

Officer Lewandowski had been on the point of dragging the woman with no licence plates, and every excuse under the sun for not having any, across the counter and throttling her. 'OK, mister, take it easy. What d'ya want?' he replied, grateful for the interruption.

'Bauer. My name is Allen Bauer. You called me a few minutes ago.'

Lewandowski's face fell. He had been hoping for a homicide at least. He turned to the busy personnel in the office behind him. 'Did any of you guys call for an Allen Bauer?' he yelled.

'Oh yeah. It's for the dumb blond,' called a young gum-chewing officer. He came out, opened the counter flap and led Allen into the waiting-room.

An assortment of drunks, druggies, bag-ladies and hookers

was lounging in the small, smoke-filled room. Allen glanced at the officer in confusion as he beckoned someone out of the crowd. But his face flickered rapidly from dismay through astonishment to a sunrise of delighted recognition as the girl in the MISS LIBERTY T-shirt walked over to him smiling.

She put her arms around his neck and devoured his readily yielding lips with hungry eagerness. When she had finished, Allen could only gaze at her, utterly oblivious of his surroundings and aware only of her fathomless blue eyes and the mysterious scent of her lithe, bronzed body.

'Hi,' he breathed at last, his mouth not moving.

Work in the precinct office had come to a complete stop.

Lewandowski walked over to them, uncertain how to proceed. 'I take it you know this girl, Mr Bauer.'

Allen's eyes were fixed on hers. 'Yeah, I do,' he murmured, his mouth still scarcely moving.

'Who the hell is she?' Lewandowski demanded, glancing down at the charge book he had picked up off the counter.

'I don't know,' Allen said, his mouth now mobile again.

Lewandowski nodded. 'Of course,' he shrugged.

The girl drew Allen's head towards her and kissed him again freely and passionately in front of the spellbound crowd of cops and vagrants.

'Miss Liberty ...' Allen whispered. 'Oh God, oh God, oh God ...' as the girl put her thigh between his and moved her leg gently against him. He closed his eyes and clung helplessly to her waist, his face buried in her hair.

Suddenly Allen's hand was seized and the damp wallet was pressed into his limp grasp.

'Get outta here both of you,' Lewandowski snarled.

With the fruit and vegetable trade light years from his mind, Allen drove Miss Liberty to his apartment block in the East Sixties. Her smiling silence did not worry him. He was too confused and nervous himself for that. Glancing sideways at her radiant face, he was struck by her insatiable interest in everything she saw as she stared around her, frowning and laughing like a child at the traffic, the buildings and the people. The events of the previous day still seemed like a dream to him, but now he was not so sure. And if it was all a dream, he certainly did not want to wake up ever again.

Tim, the liveried doorman, looked surprised to see him as he handed the outlandishly attired beauty onto the sidewalk.

'Good afternoon, Mr Bauer. You're home early today.'

'Yeah,' Allen grinned.

He showed the way through the revolving door and the girl went right round in it and re-emerged on the sidewalk, puzzled and laughing.

Allen came back out through the door to get her. 'Yeah, ah, that door... it spins, see? It spins round...' He turned to Tim. 'Get this door fixed, Timmy,' he ordered, ushering the girl back inside.

While they waited in the spacious lobby for the elevator, Allen greeted some passing neighbours with forced casualness as the girl suddenly threw her arms round his neck, pressing her firm, pointed breasts into his chest. Once again, she fed hungrily on his strong well-shaped mouth, running her hands through his hair and stirring her thigh against his hip. Allen gently tried to restrain her until the elevator arrived.

When it did, she pulled him inside the car and even before the doors had closed she unbuttoned the top of his shirt and began to caress and lick his throat and neck. Allen tried to think of some distraction to stop himself from succumbing to the overwhelming desires her onslaught provoked in him. He prayed that the elevator would not stop on its way to his floor as his body began to melt and flow in the whirlpool of surging passion that her presence created around him...

Wrapped in Allen's bathrobe, Miss Liberty gazed around the large, tastefully appointed apartment with wonder and pleasure. She spent a long time at the circular porthole in the wall, behind which multi-coloured fish swam and peered into the room with distorted globular faces. She stroked the glass lovingly, puzzled by the transparent barrier and the untouchable water. She found a glazed conch shell on a shelf of the room divider and caressed it, holding it to her cheek and listening to its hollow silence. From the kitchen, Allen's light tenor voice endlessly sang the same few phrases in full-throated happiness . . .

'O what a wonderful morning, o what a beautiful day . . .'

He came in carrying a fully laden tray balanced on the palm of one hand bent back over the shoulder like a flamboyant waiter. 'I didn't know what you liked, so I got you a choice,' he announced with a brilliant smile. 'You got here pancakes, omelettes, toast, fruit, juice . . .'

As he put the tray down on a low table the girl clung round his neck, kissing his eyes and hair and opening the front of his rumpled shirt.

'No, no, no . . .' he laughed uneasily, unwrapping her arms and leading her over to sit on the huge bed. 'I have to get back to work now,' he told her gently, kissing her forehead. He leaned across and switched on the television set. 'There. That'll keep you company while I'm gone.'

Allen picked up his tie from the floor and started knotting it. 'Now, when I come home from work in a coupla hours we'll go out and get us some dinner,' he promised her, pulling on his corduroy jacket. 'And we'll also pick up some clothes for you . . . Not that you don't look spectacular in my bathrobe.'

He bent down and kissed her again. She reached up and pulled him over the top of her, twining her long slim legs around his.

Allen struggled to free himself, but she smiled seductively and kissed him over and over again, tugging at his tie and shirt buttons.

'Bye-bye now . . .' he murmured. 'Come on now, baby, you're goin' to put me in hospital.' He finally got to his feet and glanced at his watch. 'Gee, it's gone three already. I really do have to get back to work now. You are just wonderful. Bye-bye!'

Allen went out and shut the door.

*

The girl sat disconsolately on the edge of the unmade bed staring at the television screen. On it a man was riding a horse furiously across a desert. Slowly she leaned forward and touched the screen tentatively with her fingertips. The tingle of static made her flinch away in alarm. She looked at the trayful of food and was about to go over to it when the door suddenly burst open again.

Allen rushed back into the apartment, ripping off his jacket and tie and throwing off his shoes. 'Actually things don't really get started down at the market until four o'clock...' he panted, kneeling over her thighs and sinking forward slowly as their lips closed in a long, wild kiss. Her hands tore at his shirt and dug into his back and Allen pulled her breasts out of the robe and kissed them through the cascade of thick blond hair.

Elated at the prospect of a lucrative deal with Buyrite Supermarkets, Freddie was presiding over an endless parade of onions passing on a conveyor belt and being picked over by a bored bunch of young employees. Though puzzled by Allen's strange manner and abrupt behaviour, Freddie was revelling in his new status and acting in a more and more proprietorial style around the wharf.

'Now, let's not be too choosy with these onions. Come on, you guys, some of these are perfectly good onions...' he argued as a clutch of bad ones rumbled past him. 'Hey, careful with those turnips!' he yelled as somebody dropped a tray of mangoes near by.

Just then a bright-yellow electric trolley zigzagged across the wharf and whined to a stop among the crated fruit.

'Zip-a-dee-do-da...' sang Allen boisterously, leaping off the trolley and skipping into the wharehouse like a kid in a chorus line. 'Hey, Manuel... My, oh my, what a wonderful day...'

Freddie waddled out to see what was going on.

'Plenty of sunshine heading my way,' crooned Allen, chucking a burly middle-aged wharfie under the chin. 'Zip-a-dee-do-da...' He seized a bruised mango, balanced it on his shoulder and danced his way across to his dumbfounded brother. 'Mr Mango on my shoulder,' he giggled, taking Freddie's podgy hands and whirling him round and round. 'Come on, Freddie, dance with me...'

Freddie lumbered awkwardly round, looking extremely uncomfortable. 'Wait,' he muttered. 'Hey, Allen, not in front of the teamsters.'

Allen tossed the mango to the watching wharfies. 'Hey, they're happy guys,' he cried. 'We're all happy guys.'

'You're a rotten lead,' Freddie protested, standing still while Allen pranced on solo, shouting and yodelling and clapping his hands above his head.

'Listen, Allen, I got the Buyrite contracts all ready. You wanna check them out?' Freddie bleated, trailing after his jitter-bugging brother.

Allen snatched up some spotty potatoes and started juggling them, still dancing among the bemused employees. 'No, no, no. You check 'em out, Freddie. You know the business...' he sang recklessly.

Freddie looked around the cluttered warehouse, grinning like a child with a bag of candy. 'Oh, so I'm in charge!' he cried.

'Sure you are, Freddie.'

'But what about the lawyers' meeting tonight at eight?' Freddie asked anxiously, beginning to feel a little out of his depth.

Allen spun round and round, still juggling the sick potatoes, and headed towards the stairs. 'Eight? Eight p.m.? No, no. That's too late for me,' he protested. 'Listen, Freddie, I'm going to take a nap.'

He flipped the potatoes one by one to the open-mouthed Jerry. 'Handle these for me, baby,' he said, hopping up the stairs like a hare and laughing hysterically. 'You guys just wake me when it's time to go home!' he shouted and slammed the office door.

For a while Freddie just stood there, stunned. He had not bargained for being left quite so completely in charge of Ralph Bauer & Sons. It was obviously going to be more complicated than he had realised. He waved the warehouse back to work and started to climb the stairs to the office.

10

Back in Allen's apartment, Miss Liberty was sitting naked on the bed, the remains of her brunch scattered over the low table. Occasionally she looked longingly over at the circular aquarium and the dazzling fish, but mostly she just stared in rapt fascination at the TV screen as the late-afternoon sun slatted through the half-open blinds.

'Ann Klein. Bloomingdales. Ann Klein,' insisted the TV voice as a succession of women in a variety of attire paraded up and down in front of even more women dressed in stylish clothes.

Miss Liberty glanced down at her own brown nakedness and then frowned back at the screen.

'At Bloomingdales... At Bloomingdales...' raved the voice-over.

Again she looked down at herself. Then she gazed at the MISS LIBERTY T-shirt lying crumpled in the corner of the room, then back at the elegant models magically changing from outfit to outfit with effortless ease as they mysteriously dissolved one into another.

She jumped up and ran over to the large wall-closet opposite the bed. Sliding open the doors, she revealed Allen's extensive wardrobe neatly arranged on rails and shelves.

'At Bloomingdales... At Bloomingdales...' sang the voices from the television persuasively...

Tim, the doorman, did a startled double-take as the apparition darted out of the revolving door onto the sidewalk. Then he recognised the tall beauty he had seen with Mr Bauer earlier. She was wearing one of Allen's suits. The trousers were telescoped over her bare feet, the jacket sagged off the end of each shoulder and the tie was scrappily knotted outside the flaps of the shirt collar.

She hesitated at the kerbside, glancing uncertainly up and down the street.

'Can I help you, Miss?'

She stared at Tim silently. Then her full, blooming lips moved slightly and she frowned, as if trying to remember something.

'Can't you talk?' Tim asked.

The sensuous mouth moved again, this time uttering a faint unintelligible mumble.

Tim pushed back his braided maroon cap and shook his head helplessly.

Again the lovely mouth moved. 'Bloomy dayelz...'

Tim grinned sunnily. 'Oh yeah, sure. Right away, ma'am.' And he hailed a cab and ushered the strange girl into it with ceremonious courtesy.

Outside Bloomingdales the girl got out of the taxi and left the door open as she turned to enter the bustling department store.

'Hey there, Miss...' yelled the cabbie, thrusting his large hand through the rolled-down window.

The girl looked blankly at his waggling fingers. Then she seemed to remember something. She reached into the suit, took out Allen's damp wallet and handed it over. The driver took out his fare plus a generous tip and gave it back to her.

Inside the huge store, the girl moved slowly among the counters as though in a dream. Everything she saw amazed, delighted and attracted her. In the cosmetics department she went up to the women shoppers and stared intently into their faces as they tried out the different products in front of adjustable mirrors. Oblivious of people's perplexed and occasionally resentful reactions, she moved happily through the store, gawping and fingering everything in sight.

Eventually she reached the fashion department. She

climbed onto a low plinth to examine an elegant dummy, caressing its clothes with murmurs of wonder. Then she wandered among the racks of dresses, feeling the fabrics and marvelling at the variety of colours and styles.

'Oh my God!' cried Mrs Dora Klein, the short, fifty-year-old department manageress, running over to the odd-looking customer. 'Darling, darling, darling. That outfit, it's to die from!' she exclaimed, looking the girl up and down through her diamanté glasses attached to a cord round her neck. 'What happened, darling? You saw Annie Hall a hundred times? That look is over.'

The girl smiled placidly back at her, looking critically at Mrs Klein's frothy red-and-white spotted blouse and dark tailored costume with long skirt slit to the knee. Then she went over to a nearby rack and picked out a dress at random.

'You want to try that on?' asked Dora helpfully, patting her highly styled hairdo as she passed a mirror. 'Let me assist you. Who knows . . . maybe it's you. It isn't me. I couldn't get one leg in there. My daughter on the other hand is lucky. She's anorexic.'

Chattering away, Mrs Klein led the girl over to the cubicles.

An hour later, the exhausted woman handed the girl an assortment of bags and packages together with Allen's wallet, now a little drier but also rather thinner than before. 'Please call again soon, darling,' she invited her. 'And why don't you do yourself a favour and stop by the Lingerie? A pretty girl like you shouldn't be wearing boxer-shorts!'

Now wearing a loose pale blue dress with attached scarf and a pair of squashy white turnover boots, the girl waved goodbye and resumed her wide-eyed exploration of the Aladdin's cave and its seductive treasures. In the TV department she dropped her purchases on the floor and ran over to the dozens of television sets ranged along the wall, all showing different channels and cable or movie programmes. She darted from screen to screen, devouring the endless images with hungry eyes and listening intently to the babble of unfamiliar and incomprehensible sounds.

'Colgate Winter Fresh Gel... And now we continue with Capitol... It's crazy at his greatest clearance sale ever... its crazy and he's slashing prices... stereo equipment, video equipment, telephone equipment, car stereo equipment, disco equipment... All with full manufacturers' warranty... Most prices below cost... It's crazy Eddie at his greatest sale ever at these twelve great locations – Manhattan, the Bronx, Brooklyn, Union, Westchester, Norwalk, Westbury... going on right now at prices that are insane...'

Miss Liberty watched the frenetic presenter miming manically to the strident announcements. She watched chasing cars leaping across swing bridges, strings of brilliantly flashing lights surrounding quiz-show competitors, men on horses shooting other men on horses, old people in wheelchairs getting up and walking into the arms of praying blue-suited evangelists, children talking to giant chickens and frogs... And she was quite unaware of the immaculately dressed salesman watching her in astonishment as she flitted from set to set, miming and mouthing and more and more uttering odd words and phrases back at the inexhaustible screens.

Allen bounded out of the elevator and hopped along the hallway singing and flourishing a large bunch of roses.

'Zip-a-dee-do-da... Hallo, I'm home!' he shouted, opening the front door and dancing into his apartment like a Gene Kelly hero.

Seconds later he flew back out the door and punching both elevator buttons on opposite sides of the hallway, he poised himself midway between them, silent and deathly pale. When the first car arrived he sprang into it and shot down to the lobby.

Tim was amazed to see him back outside so soon.

'I'm looking for a girl, Timmy!'

'Two hundred bucks.'

Allen looked really frightened. 'No, no, no. The one I came in with this afternoon. Remember? The blonde.'

Tim nodded slyly. 'Oh yeah. I put her in a cab.'

Allen grabbed Tim's gold-braided lapels. 'To where? Where to Timmy? Where?' he shouted frantically.

Tim thought for a moment. 'Yeah. I remember. Bloomingdales.'

Allen was gone at once. Dicing with death, he raced into the street and flailed at a passing cab. 'Halt! Stop! Hey, taxi, please!' he screamed as the traffic swerved and skidded round him on either side.

What seemed to Allen a lifetime later, he flung some cash at the driver and bolted into the entrance of Bloomingdales.

'Sir, sir, we're just closing sir,' yelled a commissionaire, making a grab for him inside the doors among the milling crowd.

'I know,' Allen yelled back, diving for the stairs. 'Just give me three minutes.'

'Come back, sir!'

'Three minutes. You can time me!' Allen screamed back over his shoulder, flying up the wide staircase three at a time like some record-seeking Olympic athlete.

Up in the television department, Miss Liberty was stretching and bending in front of the screens, her eyes glued to the Richard Simmons exercise show. Behind her at the counter, the respectable-looking manager and a young black salesman were watching her high, firm buttocks as she touched her toes energetically in time to the music throbbing from the speakers.

'She works hard for her money, so you'd better treat her right...' sang the TVs, now all showing the same channel simultaneously. 'Come on, let's go. Come on, let's go,' Simmons chanted, bullying his matronly studio participants with patronising gaiety.

The bespectacled manager cleared his throat reluctantly. 'Excuse me, Miss, but we're about to close,' he called out tentatively.

The girl carried on reaching and stretching with disciplined regularity, completely ignoring him.

'She's been here for six hours,' muttered the salesman out of the side of his mouth, without taking his eyes off the vision before him.

Eventually the manager walked up behind the girl. 'Excuse me, Miss, but I'm going to have to insist that you stop doing that,' he declared firmly.

'She works hard for her money . . .' pounded the speakers.

The manager returned to the counter. 'She's ah . . . she's exercising,' he confided quietly, as though he were imparting a mysterious secret. 'We'll, ah . . . we'll just give her a few more minutes.' And they both watched with rapt attention.

At last the manager walked slowly over to the sets and began to switch them off one by one, still eyeing the ravishing gymnast's performance with studied attention.

'Oh, thank God. Thank God . . .' cried Allen, rushing into the darkening department as the neon lights began to go out overhead. He swept Miss Liberty up in his arms and hugged her tightly, kissing her glowing cheeks and gazing into her surprised, delighted eyes with tearful relief. Murmuring softly, she bent forward and kissed his dark moist eyelids.

The manager approached. 'Do you know this woman, sir?' he enquired officiously.

'Yeah, yeah, I do,' Allen replied without looking round, clinging possessively to her vibrant body. 'I just don't know what her name is, so don't ask me.'

'Well, sir, we've been trying to explain to her that it's closing time, but she doesn't seem to understand.'

'That's because she doesn't speak any English,' Allen explained with exaggerated politeness, kissing her eyes tenderly.

'Hallo, Allen. How was your day?' Miss Liberty asked in a low, melodious voice with the tiniest trace of an accent.

Allen let go of her and stepped back in amazement.

'Excuse me,' said the manager sarcastically. 'I never went to college, but wasn't that English?'

The girl turned to him. 'Thank you for letting me use your television,' she smiled. 'It was very educational.'

The manager bowed and returned to the counter.

Allen was still gaping at her. 'What *is* your name?' he asked.

'It is hard to say in English, Allen.'

Allen shrugged. 'Well, just say it in your language,' he suggested.

She nodded. 'All right. My name is ....'

An unbearable, non-human sound of piercing high-pitched intensity sliced through the air from the girl's parted lips. Allen and the two salesmen clapped their hands over their ears, wincing with pain as the fearful noise exploded inside their heads. At the same time, the television screens exploded in showers of powdery glass, spraying sharp splinters in all directions.

In the shocked silence which followed, the three men glanced at each other in horrified disbelief and then stared round speechless at the devastation. Slowly the manager and the salesman approached the wrecked shelves, gesticulating in futile bewilderment.

Allen pulled himself together and galvanised into action. He swept the girl's packages up off the floor and grabbed her arm. 'Well... how about these dumb blondes!' he exclaimed with a nervous laugh.

Then he dragged her out of the department, down the staircase and out into the street.

11

Allen marched the girl briskly along the avenue, struggling to cope with the burden of packages she had accumulated during the afternoon's raid on Bloomingdales.

'I'm a bit confused,' he confessed. 'I mean, why haven't you said a word to me until just back there in the store?'

'I didn't know English,' she said simply.

'Oh I see,' Allen grunted, avoiding a lamp post, 'and now you do?'

'Yes, I learned this afternoon, from television. It's wonderful. Now I can ask you lots of questions and if you answer them correctly you can win one of these valuable prizes . . .'

Allen glanced sidelong at the extraordinary creature, wondering whether he was not the victim of some fiendishly elaborate hoax.

'An attractive wall clock, a matching washer-and-drier set, or a brand-new car,' she recited with apparent innocence.

Allen stopped her at a street corner where the lights were against them. 'Wait a minute, let me go first,' he protested as the passers-by thronged around them and the bright lights flashed everywhere. 'Just begin when you were born and finish up right when you blew up all the TVs.'

The sign changed from DON'T WALK to WALK.

Miss Liberty darted away from him and shinned easily up the traffic signpost. 'Pretty!' she exclaimed with childlike appreciation, fingering the buzzing green neon tubes.

Allen gazed up at her and shook his head like an indulgent parent. 'Yeah. I never really thought about it before,' he agreed, frowning and smiling at the same time. 'Are you from Cape Cod?'

She jumped nimbly down, linked arms with him and they walked on over the crossing. 'No,' she said, after a while. 'I come from another place.'

'Oh yeah. I had a cousin from there,' Allen retorted satirically. 'Are you an American?'

She laughed tantalisingly, kissing his ear. 'No.'

'So why were you at Cape Cod? Why are you in New York and why did the cops find you naked?' Allen persevered.

They were just passing three negroes playing jazz in a doorway. The girl broke away again and ran over to them excitedly. 'What's that?' she asked.

Allen joined her warily. 'The music?'

'Yes. Music. I like it. I heard some in the television, Dance Fever,' she said, gyrating sinuously to and fro in front of the buskers.

'Oh I love ya, girl . . .' sang the banjo player, coiling his hips in time with hers.

She gazed in fascination at the ridges of muscle rippling across the singer's bare stomach.

Allen tugged anxiously at her sleeve. 'Ah, hey honey, we'd best get goin' or we'll be late,' he told her firmly. 'You never heard music before today?'

She shook her head, laughing over her shoulder at the three black faces as Allen urgently walked her on.

Then all at once something caught her roving eyes across the street. 'What's that?' she cried, wriggling free and diving heedlessly into the busy traffic.

Allen closed his eyes as the howl of horns and the screech of tyres erupted all around him. There was a sickening crump and then a second one immediately afterwards. Allen opened his eyes. The girl was safe on the other side of the avenue under the glittering canopy of a cinema, gazing at the lurid posters.

'What the hell's that dame doin'?' yelled an irate cab driver.

'She coulda got me killed!' shouted another.

Allen jumped over tangled fenders and reached the opposite sidewalk in a state of trembling collapse. 'That's a movie theatre,' he gasped, clutching her shoulders and shaking like a leaf. Then he turned and faced the immobilised traffic. 'Give her a break. She's from outta town,' he spat, blindly and savagely.

'So why dontcha keep her on a leash!'

'Yeah. Yeah, and you have a nice day too,' Allen yelled.

He propelled the girl away from the hooting, shouting mêlée, and they took refuge in a pizza parlour down the next side-street.

The girl watched mesmerised while the chef twirled the huge disc of dough in the air like a bullfighter wielding his cape. 'Do you see that?' she recited. 'It's wonderfully good for you and it's so delicious too.'

Allen glanced round through the window to check if they had been pursued but there was no sign of a posse of angry cabbies. He turned to Miss Liberty. 'Listen, while you're here maybe you ought to watch a little less television,' he advised her, an edge of impatience creeping into his normally gentle voice. 'Anyhow, how long are you gonna be in town?'

She shook out her beautiful hair like a straw-coloured flame. 'Six fun-filled days.'

Allen's face fell a mile. 'Oh. Six days. Is that all?'

'Six days and the moon is full,' she nodded.

Allen pushed his face into her hair and drew her closer. The curve of her hip sent a tremor of desire through his body.

The chef looked at them enquiringly.

Allen grinned. 'Ah, just looking,' he muttered and quickly steered the ravishing girl outside.

'If I stay longer than six days I can't ever go back,' she murmured as they turned into the avenue again.

'Oh, is there some kinda immigration problem?' asked Allen, deeply troubled by this unwelcome revelation. Then he noticed that she was holding a tin mug filled with pencils standing up on end. 'Where . . . where did you get that?' he demanded, taking it roughly from her.

She pointed back towards the intersection where a blind man was feeling around in the air, his dark glasses flashing uselessly. Allen ran back and pressed the mug into the man's clawlike hand, mumbling an apology. Then he searched his pockets and put some change in the man's breast-pocket.

They walked on in silence for a while, Allen keeping his arm hooked firmly into hers and glancing covertly into the strangely radiant face with its fringe of tight corkscrew tresses.

'You know I'm goin' to have to call you something in English,' he intimated shyly, after a long look at her finely chiselled profile. 'I can't say your real name . . . whatever that was, back there in the store.'

'What are English names?'

Allen frowned. 'Well, there's millions of them I guess. There's Jennifer, Joannie, Hillary, Victoria . . .'

But she was distracted again, pulling eagerly towards a hotdog stand on a corner, attracted by the red-hot coke brazier.

'Hey, careful. Those are hot!' he warned her. 'Let's see. There's Kim and Lindy . . . Hey. Where are we now?' he suddenly exclaimed, glancing up at the street sign. 'Ah, Madison . . .'

She smiled. 'Madison?'

'Madison Avenue.'

'Madison. I like Madison,' she said, nuzzling his ear.

Allen shrugged. 'Well, you see Madison's not a name . . . Well, it is but . . .' He stopped, completely at a loss and smiled at her. 'OK. Why not? Madison it is,' he agreed. 'Good thing we weren't at 149th Street,' he laughed.

Madison stopped and looked earnestly into his dark eyes. 'Are we going back to where you live now?' she asked wistfully.

Allen grinned wryly, as though he had been putting off broaching the subject himself for a considerable time. 'Well, here's the thing,' he mumbled. 'I was goin' to find you a hotel.'

She looked at him blankly.

'But then ...' he stumbled on, 'then I figured that after this afternoon... well, I mean I just kind of assumed that we'd ...' He fell silent and gazed helplessly into her blue eyes. 'Well, would you mind coming and staying with me?' he ended up weakly.

Madison put her hand unashamedly between his taut thighs. 'But I want to stay with you,' she whispered. 'You are the reason I came here, Allen.'

Allen closed his eyes and gasped as Madison moved against him. She put her strong, slender arms round his neck and caressed his mouth with her tongue. Unaware of the traffic, the lights, the noise, the people, Allen buried his face in her breasts.

'That was a kiss ...' he murmured after a long silence.

'I know,' Madison breathed, stroking his hair and looking up into the evening sky.

Above them the brilliant moon was just a little more than half full.

That night, the moon was paler in the pre-dawn sky as Madison slipped quietly out of the bed taking great care not to waken Allen. She looked tenderly down at his peaceful face and gently pulled the sheet over his naked torso. Then she waved affectionately to the watchful fish in their illuminated aquarium across the living-room and glided noiselessly into the kitchen. She felt about in a cupboard, took out a packet and crept along to the bathroom, turning on the light and locking the door behind her.

With a tremor of excitement she opened up the taps and tipped half the salt from the packet into the bathtub. Dimming the lights to just a faint glow, she climbed into the tub and lay back with her eyes closed as the warm water swirled higher and higher around her. Mysterious moods and feelings played over her face and she uttered quiet little moans and gasps as the water rose.

Then a commotion under the water prompted her to reach up and turn off the taps. A shudder passed through her golden body and her breasts seemed to lift and swell slightly. Over the end of the bath a broad ribbed fin unfurled itself like two crescent-shaped wings and fanned out in iridescent splendour. Madison opened her eyes and gazed down happily at the delicate silver scales of her slim tail shimmering with brilliant rainbow hues in the frothing water. With a sigh of pleasure she slid down the slope of the tub and put her head under the surface, so that her hair spread like a chaste veil over her lovely form.

Allen stirred from his dream and woke. 'Madison?' he murmured into the pillow. 'I had a dream that we . . .' He sat up abruptly, peering at the rumpled empty space beside him. 'Madison, sweetheart . . .?'

With a twinge of apprehension, Allen switched on the light and got up. The fish were watching him, mouthing their eternal silent message. Then he heard the splashing of water and went through to the bathroom. 'Madison?'

There was a pause and a splash. 'Allen?'

He relaxed a little. 'Yeah. Course it's Allen. What are you doin', sweetheart?'

'I'm taking a bath'

Memories of the earlier part of the night stirred Allen's body. 'Can I come in, honey?' he murmured intimately through the door.

'No.'

Allen chuckled suggestively. 'Oh? Why not, sweetheart?'

There was a louder splash and then a tremendous thump on the bathroom floor.

Allen tried to open the door. 'What the hell was that?' he cried. 'Madison? Madison, are you all right in there?'

There was another pause.

Inside the bathroom, Madison was sitting on the bathrug hastily dabbing at her tail with a towel. 'Everything's fine,' she called,

'Well, then, let me in,' Allen told her, still uneasy.

Madison continued to dry her tail and fin with hurried,

panicky movements. 'I'll be right there Allen. I'm just changing,' she sang out reassuringly.

'Come on, Madison. Open the door. Something is wrong,' Allen shouted.

Madison reached for the hairdrier on the washbasin unit and accidentally knocked a hairbrush into the sink with a clatter. 'Oh Allen, could you make me some pancakes?'

'Make you some . . .?'

There was a sudden howl from the drier as Madison desperately tried to dry her tail.

Allen's voice became angry and determined. 'All right, Madison. Either you open this door or I'm going to break it down,' he threatened. 'This is just getting too scary.'

'No, Allen, please don't come in!' she pleaded, waving the drier up and down her tail.

'OK. That's it!' Allen shouted, heaving his shoulder against the door.

Madison grabbed the towel, covered her tail and fin and started to dry her long hair with the drier.

Allen heaved again and the lock broke off and the door flew open.

Madison looked meekly up at him. 'Hi,' she grinned.

Allen turned up the dimmer switch to full. 'Are you OK, honey?' he asked with tender concern.

'Course I am.' She turned off the drier.

'Then why wouldn't you let me in here?'

Madison gazed up and down Allen's taut, muscular frame. 'I'm shy,' she whispered seductively, grasping the towel as it stirred slightly.

Allen's fine eyebrows shot up in mock astonishment. 'Shy?' he gasped. 'You were shy? After the police station and in the car and the elevator and the bedroom and on top of the refrigerator . . . you're *shy*?'

She winked and smiled up at him. Then she drew the towel away from her legs, stood up and slipped out, touching him with her fingers as she passed. 'I was shy, Allen, yes.'

Allen looked at her long back and tumbling hair and then

shook his head at his reflection in the mirror. 'She was shy!' he echoed, switching off the light and following her into the bedroom.

12

With fanatical determination Walter Kornbluth had searched the depths of the bay for three days, convinced that he had seen what he had seen and resolved to prove it to the sceptics of the orthodox scientific establishment with whom he had waged a long-running feud concerning his wild theories. But he had failed to rediscover the elusive golden creature he had tried to photograph two days previously and now circumstances seemed to be conspiring to frustrate his mission.

He was staggering about on the seabed, blue around the lips and gasping for air, tugging frantically on his umbilical and staring through misted-up spectacles and visor at the unresponsive keel of the hired tugboat above, yelling for help and deafening himself inside the helmet.

Eventually he gave up and started hauling himself hand over hand up the sturdy air-hose. After what seemed an eternity he broke surface and ripped off his mask, gulping the fresh air as if each gulp were his last. When he had revived a little, he dragged himself up the ladder and clambered onto the deck. His two man crew were reclining in deck-chairs, one reading a tabloid newspaper with slowly moving lips, the other fast asleep in the sunshine beside the wheezing air-pump apparatus.

'Hey, brain!' Kornbluth shouted.

The elder brother woke up and opened one eye.

'You see this hose?' Kornbluth went on, shaking the bright yellow pipe at him. 'This is so I can breathe.'

The boy closed his eye and nodded his complete agreement.

'You want to get your damn deck-chair off it then?' Walter screamed breathlessly, yanking the tube which was flattened under the frame of the chair.

Lazily the lanky boy shifted the chair without even glancing down at the trapped hose.

Meanwhile his younger brother painstakingly read out a headline from the newspaper: 'BEAUTY BARES ALL AT STATUE OF LIBERTY.' The tall boy got up and wandered over to look over his shoulder.

Kornbluth divested himself of camera, knife, torch and sundry items of equipment, still breathing heavily. 'Why are you reading that stuff?' he demanded.

The boy looked up blankly. 'Ah, don't know.'

Kornbluth flung down his helmet. 'What the hell possesses the uneducated to purchase these things?' he raved, as though venting all his frustration of the past few days.

'It's interestin',' grunted the grim-faced older boy, reading the report with goggling eyes.

Kornbluth flapped across to them in his outsize scuba suit. 'You are not helping yourselves,' he castigated them severely. 'This is not news.' He snatched the tabloid from Junior. 'Gimme this. You know what's in here?' he growled. 'Nothing. You have sex. You have perversion. It's all just fabrication.' Walter flourished the photograph of Madison standing among the admiring sightseers beneath the Statue. 'Look at this, a naked woman at the Statue of Liberty,' he scoffed, flinging the paper onto the deck and stamping awkwardly back to his pile of gear. 'Where would they find a girl to do that?'

The boys grabbed the paper and studied the blooming nipples thrusting through the luscious hair. 'Right here in Cod,' grinned the younger lad, nudging his brother.

Something occured to Walter. He slithered to a halt on the slippery deck and chewed the arm of his spectacles thoughtfully. 'Here, let me see that again!' he suddenly shouted, wading back to them through the clutter of equipment and crates littering the deck.

He seized the paper and read the article quickly through a

couple of times, his black eyes glinting with eager anticipation at every line. Then he looked up at the grinning pair, his eyes fixed in a rigid stare of manic intensity.

'Take me back to the shore!' he eventually commanded in a hoarse whisper. 'Get me back to the shore. Now!'

Late that afternoon, Allen came home carrying a box wrapped in silvery gift paper and tied up in a bow with a scarlet ribbon. He peered round the front door, holding the box behind his back. To his distress he saw that Madison was sitting hunched on the bed staring at the television with tears cascading down her cheeks.

'Hey, Madison, honey. Madison, what is it?' he murmured, shutting the door and sitting down beside her. He cradled her shaking body in his arms. 'What happened?' he asked gently as she sobbed uncontrollably into his shoulder.

'It's just the saddest thing I ever saw...' she stammered out, pointing at the TV screen.

Allen glanced round. 'But it's *Bonanza*!' he laughed.

'But a man killed another man... and he... he died right in the middle of the street.'

Allen shook his head reassuringly. 'No, no, this is only television,' he explained. 'I thought you understood about TV. It's only makebelieve, honey.' Allen went over and touched the screen. 'Look, this is another pretend killing that's going on now. This guy here is an actor and next week he'll get shot in some other show, or he might shoot somebody himself... See?'

He went back and sat beside her again, stroking her face and her hair. 'When you think about it, it's kinda funny,' he grinned.

Madison stopped crying. She frowned at him. 'You mean I'm supposed to laugh?'

Allen nodded. 'Sure you are, sweetheart.'

Madison looked back at the screen and sniffed. Then she managed a little chuckle at her foolishness.

Allen leaned forward and kissed the tears from her eyes. Then he picked up the box from the bed and held it out.

'There you go. I just got you something.'

Madison took the pretty box and gazed at it fondly. Then she kissed it. 'It's beautiful, Allen. I love it,' she murmured.

Allen pointed to the scarlet bow. 'You have to open it.'

She looked surprised and even more delighted. 'There's more?' she whispered.

He nodded.

Excitedly she tore off the wrapping and opened the cardboard box. Inside was an ornamental musical-box. A miniature lady and gentleman dressed in eighteenth-century costume stood facing each other with hands joined underneath a glass dome. Allen showed Madison how to press the button on the base. There was a whirring sound and the two little figures started moving around one another in a dignified dance, while tinkling music issued from the hollow base.

Madison watched spellbound until the graceful figures gradually slowed down and stopped and the music jerked into silence. 'It's so lovely, Allen . . .' she said, her eyes shining.

He shook his head, as if unable to believe in the lithe figure in her fetching pink dress with tiny flowers sitting next to him.

He took her hand. 'So are you,' he whispered. 'So are you.'

In the evening they went out on the town and then walked hand in hand along by the river. The Hudson looked dark and forbidding as it swirled by the embankment. In a small riverside gardens they came upon a floodlit fountain consisting of a green copper mermaid perched on a rock and embracing fish. In the distance, a man was playing Bach sonatas on a battered violin. They stood and listened to the lonely melodies and watched the bright water cascading down into the basin of the fountain.

After a while, Madison asked Allen if he liked the fountain, as if she sensed that it was a special landmark for him.

'Yeah, I do,' he said. 'I don't know why really. Just somethin' about it. It always appealed to me ever since I was a kid.'

Madison nestled closer to him. 'Do you like the sea, Allen?'

He thought for a few moments. 'No, I don't. When I was about eight years old I had this accident. It was on a boat and I...'

'Yes, I remember,' she told him, very quietly.

Allen pulled away slightly and stared at her. 'What?'

Her face was in shadow. 'No, I mean ... I forget the words,' Madison went on hurriedly. 'I mean I understand,' she corrected herself, smiling apologetically. 'Did you get hurt?'

'No, I didn't. I was lucky ...' Allen murmured, a faraway look creeping into his eyes as he gazed at the copper mermaid on her rock. 'But when I was under the water I thought...'

'Yes?' she breathed, almost sighing wistfully.

'I could've sworn I saw ... I saw ...'

'What did you see Allen?'

He shook his head. 'Nothing. It was nothing.' He moved away, hands thrust in pockets, as if he were trying to forget rather than trying to remember. 'I was just a stupid kid,' he insisted.

Madison followed him round the shimmering basin beneath the fountain.

'You know, they're going to destroy this park,' Allen suddenly burst out angrily. 'They want to build some load of river front apartments or some such nonsense. Tear all this out.' He gestured round the little park and shrugged.

Madison glanced back at the jade-coloured mermaid on her rock. Allen seemed preoccupied and remote. She slipped her hand in his once more.

'Hey honey, what do you want to do now?' he grinned, coming to life again. 'You want to go home?'

Madison glanced up at the moon hanging over the World Trade Centre. She saw, with regret, that it was a little fuller than last night. She shook her head emphatically. 'No, Allen, I have five days left.'

Allen turned suddenly to grasp her slim shoulders with possessive hands. 'No, no, sweetheart. I mean my home. Home with me,' he said tenderly.

Madison fondled his ears and they kissed.

'Yes,' she said. 'Home.'

Allen had forgotten about the moon, but he was on the brink of asking about the five days left business and all the many other things he did not understand. But gazing into Madison's eyes, he wasn't sure whether he wanted or needed to understand. Not yet anyway.

And then she kissed him again. And the man played Bach until they went home.

13

Next morning, Allen met Freddie at the Racquets Club. His big brother talked endlessly about his plans for the business as he struggled out of his suit, hustling and bustling with ambition. By contrast, Allen had been letting his grip on Ralph Bauer & Sons slip badly during the past two days and he felt guilty but helpless in the face of Madison's relentless attractions.

'Why do we want to go to some goddam political dinner?' Allen demanded, as they changed in the locker-room for their squash game.

Freddie zipped up the front of his purple tracksuit and patted his stomach comfortingly. 'Because the President will be speaking there, that's why,' he explained, picking up his half-smoked cigar off the radiator.

Allen dragged himself out of his tight jeans. 'The president of what?'

Freddie rested his small head against the metal door of the locker and gently banged it. 'The President of the United States!'

Allen pulled on some snazzy silk shorts. 'No kidding?'

Freddie loomed closer and winked. 'We'll be rubbin' shoulders with the big shots I tell ya,' he confided. 'You think big, you be big.'

Allen glanced significantly at Freddie's vast frame stretching the tracksuit zips almost to breaking. 'I guess so,' he admitted grudgingly. He went on changing in silence while Freddie puffed dreamily at his cigar and fiddled with the cooler-box he'd brought, stacked full of Budweiser.

'Listen, Freddie, would you mind if I took Madison to this dinner thing instead of goin' with you?' Allen asked eventually.

His brother burst into a raucous roar of laughter. Freddie clutched at his heart with both hands. 'Somethin' in here's not workin'...' he mocked. 'Oh I'll never fall in love, Freddie. I can't. It won't work with me...' he cried, capering like a vaudeville lover.

Allen laced up his sports shoes. 'Who said anything about me being in love?' he snapped.

Freddie snorted. 'Ha! You haven't bin to work for two days!'

'That's an exaggeration.'

'Admit it, baby...' Freddie insisted gleefully.

'No,' Allen snapped petulantly.

Freddie suddenly reached out and grabbed him in a playful headlock and they careered around the echoing locker-room like a couple of all-in wrestlers.

'The Eye Gouge!' Freddie announced dramatically, miming with his stubby fingers. 'Come on. Admit it.'

'No.'

'The Bone Crusher!' Freddie threatened.

Allen fell to the floor, feigning death.

Ten minutes later they were battling it out in the squash court. Behind the glass wall, fashionably kitted-out cognoscenti watched them with sour, humourless contempt as they lounged about with fruit juices.

Allen darted nimbly all round the court, while Freddie lumbered around in the middle with a cigar clamped between his teeth, swinging viciously at every ball and breathing like an ancient steam locomotive.

After a while, Freddie staggered back against the wall, his sweat-band resembling a collapsed halo. 'How long we bin playin'?' he panted.

'About five minutes,' Allen replied chirpily, diving for a difficult return.

'Oh God...' Freddie gasped, blowing through the cigar

and bending down to reach into the cooler-basket in the corner. 'My heart's beatin' like a rabbit. Ya want a beer?'

'No thanks.'

Freddie unzipped the can and swigged mightily away, seating himself thankfully on the lid of the cooler and watching Allen thrusting and parrying with lithe grace on his own.

'So tell me this, Allen . . .' Freddie puffed. 'If you're not in love with that girl, why do all these little things she does drive you so goddamed crazy?'

Allen reached, missed the ball and then wandered over to him in the corner. '*Little* things Freddie?' he protested. 'The girl learned to speak English in a single afternoon.'

Freddie shrugged. 'So? She probably could speak English already. I think she must've been in shock from bein' arrested.'

Allen retrieved the ball and served stylishly. 'Well, what about that, Freddie? I mean what about a woman showing up naked in a public place?' he challenged, making a split-second shot behind his back.

Freddie smiled broadly. 'Well, I'm all for it, of course.' Perched on the cooler, he watched Allen punishing himself while he puffed and swigged noisily. 'You said she had some kinda immigration problem,' he brooded. 'Maybe she was on an ocean liner in the middle of the Atlantic and she sees America and it looks good . . . So she greases her body up like some Channel swimmer and dives in . . . She goes through some sharks maybe . . . trouble there . . . goes through the coastguard and some minefields . . . and then she's on shore and she's OK . . . Miss Liberty,' Freddie concluded triumphantly.

Allen smashed ball after ball round the walls, emphasising his words with each powerful stroke.'Well . . . what about the bathtub, and the moon stuff, and what about all those TVs . . .?'

Freddie brooded again. 'OK. I'm bein' serious,' he resumed morosely. 'I mean I've had a few fiascos in my own love life and . . .'

Allen stopped in his tracks, leaving the ball to rocket off the walls until it finally trickled into a corner. 'Freddie, you took a date to one of your own weddings,' he shouted derisively.

His brother glared up at him. 'Know what your problem is, my son? You're in love with the girl and you're tryin' to convince yourself you're not.'

Allen stood in front of him, his arms hanging loosely, shaking his head in despair. 'I just don't know, Freddie . . . it's something about it that just isn't right, that's all,' he mumbled.

Freddie heaved himself to his feet and lumbered over to get the ball. 'I'll serve. You hold the beer,' he suggested. 'That'll be your handicap.'

Allen took the can absently. 'Oh, we're gonna play?'

'Yeah. I'm goin' to teach you a lesson in humility,' Freddie told him. He lined himself up to serve, his chubby face set with the concentration of a champion, carefully judging the shot. 'OK. Humility. One on one. All set?'

Allen skipped lightly on his toes in readiness. 'Yeah.'

'Then here we go . . .' Freddie hit the ball a blistering thwack. It rebounded viciously, flew back and hit him in the head like a shell. Freddie groaned with disappointment and keeled over onto his face like a huge soft toy bear.

At that very moment, in the American Museum of Natural History just across the city, an ugly confrontation was taking place in the conference room. Despite the sober, rational atmosphere evoked by the tall arched windows, the massive polished mahogany table with its rows of turquoise-shaded, brass, art nouveau lamps and the glass-fronted book and specimen cases lining the walls from floor to ceiling, tempers were melting and voices cracking with angry indignation.

At the bottom of the table stood Walter Kornbluth, dressed in green corduroy suit, checked shirt and woollen tie. He was staring fixedly at the two rows of figures seated down either side of the table, at American, European, African and Oriental faces, both male and female, all of them alert and reasonable and, above all, expert. At the far end, seated at the head of the august assembly was Dr Ross, the Curator of Palaeontology. Ross was sharp and acid, with pale grey eyes, a clipped grey moustache and a grey suit. His bow-tie was a ghastly green.

Ross had listened to Kornbluth until he could listen no longer. He peered at the impudent upstart at the other end of the table, his mouth twisted in a tight warp of contempt. 'So this is what we all came to hear?' he exclaimed in a dry, rasping voice. 'You call us and you tell us that you have made a discovery that will stretch the frontiers of Palaeontology and Zoology with epoch-making certainty . . .' The voice began to rise and sharpen. 'And we all interrupt important and serious work to fly here at a moment's notice . . .' The voice reached a shrill, corrosive intensity. 'And today you give us . . . you give us *mermaids*?'

All heads turned to stare at Kornbluth showing masks of outrage, pity and stupefaction. There was a chasm of silence in the vast chamber.

Then Dr Ross sprang to his feet. He was a surprisingly short man. 'Don't call us,' he hissed malevolently down the gleaming blade of mahogany, call *That's Incredible*!' And with that he snatched up his briefcase and marched tight-lipped out of the room.

As the other academics followed Ross in hostile silence, Walter realised that a solitary man had remained seated midway along the table. The man was staring at Walter over his half-moon spectacles, his unkempt silver hair and permanently raised eyebrows giving him an other-worldly appearance. The man wore a shabby cardigan and a lapsed bow-tie. Under the table he sported a pair of carpet slippers.

He watched Walter sink slowly into his chair and bury his face in his hands. Then he got up and shuffled down the empty, echoing conference chamber towards him. 'What happened to you, Kornbluth? You were the brightest student in my class,' he recalled in a weary, disillusioned voice. 'True, emotionally you were only twelve years old.'

'Professor Zidell, I *was* only twelve years old,' Walter

retorted through his fingers.

'That's right. That's right, Walter. And look what you've turned into. A schmuck!'

Walter remained motionless. 'There is a mermaid in New York City,' he stated categorically.

Professor Zidell picked up the copy of the *Cape Cod Courier* from the pile on the table in front of his disgraced ex-student. 'You mean this naked girl here? Well, how come this mermaid's got legs?'

Walter's head snapped upright. 'She has legs out of the water. She has fins in the water,' he shouted. 'You taught me that, Professor, don't you remember? You taught me all the legends. You used to bring me into your office and show me those charts on the wall of where sailors had reported they saw mermaids.'

Professor closed his eyes and made a kind of sighing noise between his gold teeth. 'Walter, that was just for fun,' he explained patiently. 'It was for relaxation. Not for you to build your whole life on.' Walter jumped up, snatching the *Courier* from Zidell's frail grasp and the other newspapers from the table. 'I am gonna prove to you and all those other intellectual dinosaurs that the girl is a mermaid!' he vowed hoarsely, turning and making for the door.

'How?' the Professor called sceptically after him. 'Are you going to get her wet so that everyone sees she's really got fins?'

Walter paused with his hand poised over the ornate brass door-handle shaped like a mermaid. Then he smiled secretively and rushed out of the museum.

14

That afternoon, Allen came home early again and as he walked out of the lift, whistling cheerfully, he was surprised to see the door to his apartment wide open. Workmen in overalls were backing out with a small trolley and some light scaffolding was piled in the hallway outside. Allen ran down the hallway, his carefree expression abruptly replaced by a grim look of foreboding.

Madison looked startled and then overjoyed to see him as she met him in the doorway wearing a dazzling white trouser-suit which added a touch of elegance to her wild beauty.

'Allen... you're home!' she sang out, embracing him fiercely on the threshold.

Allen gestured around him in bewilderment. 'What the hell's goin' on round here, sweetheart?' he gasped.

Madison put her hands over his eyes. 'I got you a present, Allen,' she whispered tantalisingly. 'But don't look. Promise you won't look,' she warned him.

'What? Well, just wait a...' Allen stuttered as a vast labourer covered in dust squeezed past, winking knowingly at him. 'Listen honey, I gotta close the door...'

Madison grasped the collar of his windcheater and drew him seductively into the apartment.

'What are you doing?' he protested, kicking the door shut with his foot. 'All right, I won't look.'

Madison took his hands. 'Promise,' she whispered.

Allen promised, closing his eyes and following her impatiently through into the bedroom area. He heard the mysterious splashing of water. 'Are we goin' to take a bath?' he asked.

Madison paused. 'Okay Allen, you can look now.'

Allen opened his eyes. Almost immediately he shut them again and gasped. Then he opened them. There was a long silence. 'Yeah,' he finally managed to croak, 'yeah, well, that's . . . that's big. It's really big. And it's really here!'

In front of him, taking up most of the living-room, was the copper mermaid fountain from the gardens, complete with the basin and water streaming down the statuary.

Allen sat heavily on the edge of the bed and stared at the prodigious gift, assuming that in a moment or two he would mercifully wake up from this nightmare. Madison knelt behind him and put her arms round his shoulders and her head against his, anxiously waiting for his approval.

'It's . . . it's just so . . . so big!' he laughed nervously, still stunned.

'You told me they were going to tear it down so I bought it for you,' Madison told him. 'It's yours now.'

Allen blinked and nodded and gulped. 'Honey, where did you get the money to pay for a thing like this?' he murmured, the brutal reality of the thing only just beginning to sink in.

Madison kissed the top of his head and kept silent.

Allen felt her breasts against his shoulder blades and then realised something was missing. 'Madison . . . not your beautiful necklace?' he cried, twisting round to look. Her neck was bare.

She nodded solemnly. 'I traded it for the statue.'

'Why sweetheart? Why?'

'Because I love you Allen.'

He got up and slowly walked round the statue, trailing his fingers in the water. The jade-coloured mermaid smiled down at him as he watched the water dripping from her breasts. He smiled up at her familiar face. Then he rushed over and knelt beside Madison.

'Listen, Madison, I love the present. I love the present and I love you,' he murmured fervently, taking her delighted face and kissing it all over and laughing with all his heart.

'And I love you,' she whispered. As they kissed again, her eyes wandered to the mermaid and a wistful sadness passed over her face. She drew a little away from him as if to tell him some painful thought that had just come into her mind. Allen smiled back enquiringly. But Madison kept silent, her fingers beginning to undo the buttons of his shirt as he slipped the jacket from her shoulders, murmuring quietly.

A little persistent enquiring plus a few dollars distributed shrewdly here and there at the precinct headquarters and at the newspaper offices had yielded information which had led Walter Kornbluth to park his car across the street from Allen's apartment. Now he was waiting for his prey, tense with expectation. Behind him on the floor in the back of the car sat two tin buckets filled with water and covered with lids.

At long last Allen and Madison emerged and got into a cab. Walter trailed them across to Fifth Avenue where they paid off the driver outside St Patrick's Cathedral and set out on foot northwards towards the Park. Walter kerb-crawled along behind them as they window-shopped in innocent oblivion. Near Tiffanys the couple wandered into a shoe store and Walter parked illegally near by. Slinging a 35mm camera and lens cases round his neck, he scrambled out, dodging the dense traffic passing around the obstruction he had created.

Keeping one eye on the bustling sidewalk outside the crowded shops, he opened the rear offside door, knocked the lids off the buckets and hauled the brimming pails out of the car. Kicking the door shut, he staggered round onto the sidewalk, weighed down into a Groucho Marx posture and fought his way through the passers-by just as the blue-coated, long-haired girl on the arm of the grey-flannelled and blue-blazered young man came out of the shop and turned along the Avenue towards Tiffanys.

Slopping water right and left, Kornbluth stumbled between the elegant shoppers keeping his eyes glued to his quarry as they stopped and admired the displays in Tiffanys' famous windows. He crept up close behind them, put down one bucket, flung the contents of the other bucket over the girl's legs and quickly repeated the routine with the first bucket. Then, with buckets clattering and rolling around his feet, he snatched up the camera and focused with fiendish concentration on the girl's dripping wet knees.

With a startled scream the girl turned round. So did her escort. Kornbluth waited excitedly, forefinger poised over the button, the shapely calves sharply in focus in his viewfinder. But nothing happened. The expected metamorphosis failed to occur. Then everything went momentarily black as a large hand wrenched the camera from his grasp. Walter found himself staring at a thick-necked quarterback with a broken nose, who seized him by the throat and shook him.

'Hey, what d'ya think ya doin', four eyes?' bellowed the man.

In the background Walter just glimpsed a completely unfamiliar girl in a blue coat. She was sobbing with shock and indignation.

'Oh my God, oh my God!' Walter stammered, clutching frenziedly at his assailant's fingers in a vain attempt to prise them off his windpipe.

Then everything seemed to whirl crazily round and round and up and down while voices yelled and laughed and gigantic metal bells clanged against his head. Finally, everything went black again with a sickening thud.

15

Totally unaware of their narrow escape that afternoon, Allen and Madison ended up in a smart, rather pretentious restaurant close to the Rockefeller Centre for an early dinner. Allen sat toying with the cutlery, preoccupied and silent. Madison was, as usual, taking in her surroundings with unflagging and alert perceptiveness. Happily she fingered the tasteful modern necklace Allen had bought her at Tiffanys to replace the beautiful treasure she had sacrificed in her desire to make him love her and she kept turning round to attract the attention of neighbouring diners to her new adornment. In her low-cut pink dress with tiny flowers and matching wrap she looked quite ravishing.

Now and again she gazed at Allen, puzzled by his remoteness, but uncertain how to woo him out of it. There were still so many things she did not understand about the new world she found herself increasingly at home in, and she desperately wanted to avoid causing unhappiness by behaving in the wrong way.

While they waited for the entrée, Allen balanced a teaspoon on his finger and tapped the end of the handle, seeing how far he could make it swing without falling off. Suddenly there was a flash of bright metal and a clatter as the spoon flew across the tables and hit the wall between an elderly couple who were eating snails in a corner.

'Ooops...' Allen said, with an insolent grin as mild protests rose around them. 'Nice earrings!' he called over to the woman, whose ears were sagging with hideous Victorian ironmongery.

The couple glared back over their *Escargots à la Nixon.*

Madison took Allen's restless fingers in hers. 'Is there something wrong?' she murmured.

He smiled with artificial readiness. 'No, no. Nothing at all,' he replied unconvincingly.

There was a pause. Allen fidgeted again.

'You know I was thinking, Madison, you don't have to leave this country,' he told her eventually.

'Yes, I do.'

'No, no, no . . . You see there's all kinds of stuff we can do,' Allen assured her earnestly, with more than a touch of desperation in his voice. 'I mean, to get round the immigration laws. For instance, I could give you a job down at the market. We could get you a work permit.' He paused, searching Madison's face for some sign of assent or approval. 'Then you could . . . well, marry. Like marry an American. Then they'd have to let you stay,' he added in a sudden eager rush of words, seizing her hands.

A fleeting look of regret passed over Madison's serene face as she listened. She kept looking up from his hands into his face as if she were on the brink of revealing something. But Allen interpreted her hesitant silence as a refusal. He shook his head defeatedly, as if struggling to banish tears.

Just then the over-dressed bogus French waiter wheeled up their dinner on a trolley.

'Look, our food is here!' exclaimed Madison, gazing hungrily at the two glazed lobsters with sudden enthusiasm.

Allen grinned bravely. 'Oh well, I guess we can talk about it later,' he sighed.

The obsequious waiter served them with elaborate gestures. 'Do be careful, Madame,' he pouted, 'these plate is very 'ot.'

Allen waved him away. 'Thank you. These look terrific.'

Madison picked up her lobster entire and took an enormous bite, crunching right through the shell. Allen stared at her in amazement. She grinned back, murmuring appreciatively as she devoured the flesh and the shell together.

Allen glanced around in acute embarrassment. Gradually the other diners had stopped eating and were sitting gaping at the extraordinary woman as she proceeded to tear the lobster apart with her flashing teeth in wild relish.On the dais, the black pianist played slower and slower with a rash of wrong notes. Waiters turned in mid-flourish and goggled incredulously at the crackling crunching beauty with the long hair and the thrusting breasts. Allen picked up his fork and tinkered with his own food as if nothing unusual were happening. But the noise Madison was making could not be ignored.

He grinned and nodded casually at the adjacent tables, gesturing with his fork and shaking his head at Madison. 'Boy . . .' he intimated wryly, 'boy, is she hungry!'

Madison nodded earnestly at him in reply and attacked the remains of her crustacean with even more furious gusto, wiping her mouth with the back of her hand and licking her fingers as she consumed every last morsel on her plate.

After dinner they went to a small outdoor skating rink near the United Nations Building. Allen led Madison carefully onto the ice, but she soon slipped his grasp and took off solo, gliding and turning with effortless ease, her pink cheeks charmingly matching the colours in her billowing dress. She reminded Allen irresistibly of the lithe lady on the musical-box as they met and separated, approached and departed in the cold night air, like figures in a fairy story. He was astonished at Madison's graceful skill, which was quite baffling in an apparent beginner. Several times he stopped and watched her open-mouthed as she pirouetted brilliantly for his benefit among the dozen or so other skaters.

They sat down for a breather on one of the benches. 'Hey, baby, you are very, very good,' Allen murmured, his face shining with admiration.

Madison kissed him and he held her close for a moment. 'Let's you and me talk,' he suggested gently.

'Your nose is cold,' she teased, as if to distract him.

He tweaked her chin. 'I don't want to talk about my nose.'

She burst into peals of laughter, pointing at his head. 'Your ears are all red,' she giggled.

Allen squirmed self-consciously. 'I don't want to discuss any part of myself,' he warned her severely.

Madison fell silent and looked serious suddenly.

'But I do want to talk about what happened back there in the restaurant.'

There was a long pause. Madison bowed her head guiltily. At last she looked up. 'I'm sorry, Allen. That's how we eat lobster where I come from,' she said shamefacedly.

'No, no, no, I don't care about that,' Allen retorted. 'No. You see I was trying to do something back there and I guess I did it very badly.' He hesitated, glancing at the happy throng of skaters. 'I was trying to ask if you . . . if you wanted to get married?'

Madison sat gazing up at the nearly rounded moon as streamers of cloud trailed across it. She said nothing.

Allen took her face in his hands. 'Madison, will you marry me?'

She shook her head immediately. 'No.'

Allen slowly took his hands way, staring at her with dulled eyes. 'What? Just no? You don't want to think about it . . . about what I just asked you? Weigh the pros and cons? You don't want to kick it around for a while . . .?' he exclaimed sarcastically.

She looked away. 'I can't marry you, Allen.'

'Why not?'

'I can't tell you.'

Allen stared bleakly at the skaters for a while. 'Look, I know you think you have some great big secret you think you can't tell me . . . But you can tell me,' he persisted.

Madison kept silent.

'What is it? You're already married?'

'Allen . . .'

'Or you're dying. You're gay? You're crazy? You were once a man? Whatever it is, I don't care. You can tell me.'

She turned to him in a panic, her eyes glistening. 'Allen, I only have three days left. Please make them wonderful,' she implored.

At last he turned back to her. 'OK,' he said simply.

'Want to skate some more?'

He nodded.

Madison glided thankfully out onto the ice and performed a series of spectacular pirouettes for him. But Allen blatantly ignored her and stood virtually still, watching a couple of about sixty skating sedately and joyfully around the rink.

Madison executed a clever turn beside him. 'You know those people?' she asked.

'No,' Allen replied, still watching them. 'I've just seen them here before. I guess they've been coming here together for about forty years.'

She watched them. 'They look very happy,' she murmured.

Allen swung abruptly round on her. 'Well now, why shouldn't they be happy?' he demanded harshly. 'They get to spend their whole lives together, don't they?'

Allen skated furiously away from her, bombing recklessly round the ice close to the wooden barriers. Madison set off after him and quickly caught him up.

'Is this really what happens to water when it gets cold?' she asked, as if nothing had happened between them.

'Yeah.'

'Where I come from it never gets cold,' she laughed.

'Hey, well what a break for wherever that is,' Allen snapped viciously.

Madison glided back to the benches and sat down again. Suddenly she looked alone and vulnerable. Allen did a few more circuits, gradually calming himself down. Then he skated over to her.

'You know you just really opened up to me back there,' he told her. 'You opened up for the first time.'

Madison was tugging at the laces of her skates. 'Your voice sounds funny,' she mumbled, blushing brightly.

Allen stood over her, hands on hips. 'Yeah, well it's called sarcasm,' he spat brutally. 'But I suppose they don't have that where you come from either.'

'No . . .' she whimpered, fighting back the tears as she pulled off the skates.

Allen glared down at her, determined to hurt her. 'They don't have ice. They don't have music. They don't have sarcasm. Just what kind of a goddam place is it, Madison?' he shouted.

Throwing the skates down, Madison jumped up and ran quickly out of the rink enclosure. Yelling her name over and over again, Allen tried to go after her, tottering clumsily on the skates. But she didn't pause or even glance back at him once. As he reached the admission booth, the attendant grabbed his arm.

'Hey, Mac, those skates are rented!'

Allen wriggled free. 'Just give me one second . . .' he shouted aggressively, tripping over the skates as he stumbled through the turnstile and clattered after the swiftly running figure in the distance. 'Madison . . . Madison . . . I'm sorry, sweetheart . . .' he yelled pathetically.

Next moment the attendant had brought him down with a flying tackle and they were rolling along the boardwalk struggling viciously.

The attendant started to untie the skates. 'Let her go, Mac,' he advised sourly. 'Show some dignity, for chrissakes . . .'

But Allen was aware only of the fleeing figure of his precious lady from the sea, receding irretrievably from his grasp into the night as spots of rain began to fall, pattering more and more thickly until they formed into a torrential downpour.

Overhead, the moon was hidden from human eyes.

16

Allen had no idea how long he roamed the streets searching for Madison. He ran first to his apartment block, but Tim had not seen her. Then he ran to the local police station, but the officers there, busy coping with drunks, muggers, sniffers, suicides and traffic accidents couldn't help him at all. A lot of the time he just walked as though in a trance, colliding with pedestrians and narrowly escaping death whenever he suddenly decided to dart across the street. He even stopped people at random to ask if they had seen her. 'Yeah, you know, the Miss Liberty girl . . .' Of course, everyone and no one had seen her. The whole city seemed to have turned to liquid, merging and flowing swiftly down the drain of Time. He was soaked through, but he never noticed. He just kept on searching.

In the small hours, he found himself on the waterfront. He crossed a footbridge somewhere down among the wharves and stopped in the middle, staring down into the black water. Over the opposite rail, harbour lights endlessly mingled their reflections in the heaving surface, their ever-changing pictures telling stories in the water. Suddenly Allen remembered the river-cruiser at Cape Cod twenty years before and the pictures in the water then. He remembered the feeling of isolation from the world and the lure of the pictures in the water.

The urge to climb onto the rail and jump coursed through his body like cold blood. Only apathy and exhaustion stopped him succumbing to it now. He roused himself and wandered on.

*

Not far away, under the arches of the road-bridge, Madison had been sheltering for hours from the lethal rain. She bitterly regretted her sudden flight from the rink, but she felt unable to resolve the cruel conflict inside her concerning Allen and the future. Safe from the lashing torrent endlessly falling out of the graphite skies, she gazed into the swirling waters of the East River, desperately trying not to acknowledge the terrible truth it was telling her. After abandoning Allen, she had run from tree to tree and from awning to awning to escape the rain, lost without the pale disc of the moon with both its comfort and its reminder of the coming sadness.

The sea had seemed to draw her inexorably back to it and now there seemed to be only one way for her to go. Slowly she unbuttoned her dress. Already the dampness of her hair was reassuring, a taste of the familiar world again. Her resolution began to harden. She walked to the edge of the wharf. The heaving water called to her. She moved forward, opening her dress.

All at once she became aware that she was not alone after all. Someone was sitting on the wharf half-hidden by one of the buttresses of the road bridge, legs dangling over the edge. The dark hair was flattened and plastered to the head, making the ears stick out and the clothes clung tightly to the lean body, which was shaking silently and uncontrollably.

Madison hesitated. She looked at the dark water. She looked at Allen. She walked slowly towards Allen.

'Allen,' she called softly.

There was silence. Allen stopped crying. Madison stood beside him.

'What?' Allen murmured. He didn't move or look up. He seemed lost in a dream.

'Yes,' she said.

For a long time nothing happened. Then slowly Allen reached out and put his arms around her legs and held her. After a while he knelt up and hugged her hips and pressed his head into her lap. Madison leaned over him and her breasts brushed his face. He stood up and they held each other under the bridge, while the rain petered out into odd flurries and the swelling moon lurked dull and pasty behind the thinning cloud high over the murmuring city.

They wandered happily and aimlessly through the damp, gleaming Manhattan streets, aware only of each other. Allen was animated, chattering incessantly, laughing and joking and being suddenly serious. Madison walked arm in arm beside him, enjoying his boyish vigour and his fun, but bearing within her the burden of the secret which she had been on the brink of taking away with her forever into the ebbing tidewaters beneath the bridge.

Allen turned to her excitedly. 'See, I mean if we get our blood tests done today we can be married as early as tomorrow,' he suggested. 'I mean if we wanted to,' he added with transparent tact.

Madison smiled indulgently. 'Allen, before we get the blood tests done I shall have to tell you everything,' she insisted.

Allen spread his arms with carefree abandonment. 'So tell me everything, sweetheart,' he shouted recklessly, spinning along the kerb like a top.

Madison pressed her lips together with uncharacteristic firmness and shook her head. 'Not today,' she said playfully.

Allen clung to her arm like a child pestering its mother for some toy or treat. 'But see here, honey . . . if we get the tests done today . . . no pressure on you, baby . . . then, well, that's that all done and as soon as you tell me, we can get married. Anytime, see?'

Madison just smiled enigmatically. Allen smiled too and fell silent for a while.

Eventually they reached the apartment building.

'You are just goin' to love bein' married to me,' Allen started on again as they came through the revolving door. 'I just so happen to come from a long line of married people . . .'

He broke off momentarily to wish good morning to a hunchbacked one-armed janitor who was half-heartedly washing the marble floor of the lobby with a bucket and mop. The janitor grunted without turning round.

'My Mom and Dad, they were married . . .' Allen buzzed as they entered the elevator, 'and their moms and dads, they were married too,' he revealed intimately, as though passing on some terrible secret.

Madison dissolved into melodious laughter at Allen's bubbling repartee as the elevator doors closed behind them.

The janitor straightened up and flung down his mop. It was Walter Kornbluth. His left arm was encased in a thick plaster cast and it stuck out at an angle under his borrowed overall, supported on a stainless steel surgical bracket fixed round his waist. Behind his cracked glasses, one eye was lividly discoloured and his lower lip was swollen angrily.

As soon as the elevator doors had closed, he slithered across the wet floor and started running up the carpeted staircase two steps at a time. At each landing he glanced up at the indicator to check that he was ahead of the car. Reaching the fourth floor with the indicator showing 3, Walter raced across the hallway to a potted plant, snatched a camera from the foliage and slung it round his neck. Then he smashed the glass front of a fire-hose panel with his armoured left elbow and raced back towards the elevator, unreeling the fire hose behind him.

As the indicator reached 4 and the doors opened, Walter opened the valve and a thin jet of high-pressure water shot into the lift. He sprayed the jet up and down and from side to side as if it were a barrage of machine-gun fire, while screams and shouts of dismay issued from the flooded car. After a few seconds he turned off the valve, flung down the hose and aimed the camera at his victims, clicking frantically away. As the mist on his spectacles cleared, Walter's eye widened in horror in the viewfinder.

'You son of a bitch,' bellowed a drunken male voice as a hulking young man advanced out of the elevator clenching and unclenching his fists in a frenzy of indignation. Behind him, a pretty brunette in an evening gown was blowing her matted hair out of her mouth and uttering piercing shrieks of terror and shock.

Seconds later, Walter Kornbluth was cartwheeling down the staircase towards the lobby with the fire hose wrapping itself tighter and tighter round his body.

'I though we were going upstairs...' Madison exclaimed as the doors opened and Allen led her back into the lobby and towards the street.

'Yeah, I know, honey,' he replied, stopping and taking her by the shoulders. 'But I love you. I love you and I'm not gonna lose you again.' He guided her towards the revolving door. 'So we are getting married tonight. We're gonna get in the car and we're gonna drive down to Maryland,' he informed her firmly. 'I don't know why I didn't think of it before. Freddie always gets married in Maryland. You don't need a blood test down there...'

Suddenly Allen stopped in his tracks. 'Damn! There's this dinner tomorrow night with the President,' he remembered, slapping himself on the forehead. 'Hey, but that's OK! We can drive down to Maryland after we have dinner with the President,' he exclaimed, brightening up again and leading the bewildered Madison back to the elevator. 'We'll even be dressed up already, sweetheart.'

Madison looked uneasy as they got back into the lift. 'Allen, I still haven't told you about my...'

'I know. I know, sweetheart. You haven't told me this great big dark secret of yours,' Allen grinned, pressing the fourth floor button. 'That's OK. You can tell me in the car on the way to Maryland.'

As the doors closed, moans of pain and frustration echoed round the lobby from the direction of the staircase as Walter Kornbluth extricated himself from the tangled fire hose and examined the remains of his precious camera. Then he dragged himself out of the building and into his car and retreated to plan the next assault in his campaign to expose the secret mermaid of New York. And next time he was determined to succeed.

17

Most of the next day Allen and Madison slept and made love and slept and made love, while the fountain trickled musically and the mermaid smiled down on them protectively. Allen answered a few vague enquiries on the telephone from Mrs Stimler and banished the business from his mind again. In the evening, he and Madison got dressed up for the presidential dinner and for the trip to Maryland afterwards. He put on an immaculate tuxedo and she donned a long dark blue dress in the Grecian style and brushed her hair freely over her honey shoulders. Allen fixed the necklace he had bought for her the day before round her neck and they set off.

The dinner was a dazzling occasion. Limousine after limousine purred up to the hotel entrance. Furs and jewels and medals gleamed in the lights as press and television captured the rich and the powerful and the ambitious parading into the glittering lobby. Madison glowed with excitement as they drove up in Allen's smart BMW and she was handed out onto a long red carpet by a uniformed valet.

As they sat down at their table in the vast banqueting hall hung with huge crystal chandeliers and mountains of flowers, Allen leaned across to her grinning like a child. 'You know what I hope?' he murmured tenderly. 'I hope we have a boy and a girl.'

Madison gazed in awe at the hundreds of guests seated at round tables. 'What kind?' she whispered, as a waiter filled their glasses.

Allen chuckled happily. 'What kind? Well, the young kind

I guess, sweetheart. The older kind are a little troublesome to deliver.' He picked up his glass and turned to their neighbours. 'We're getting married tonight!' he announced.

The other guests called out congratulations and raised their glasses in a toast.

'Oh, thank you,' Allen cried, smiling radiantly at Madison and drinking heartily.

Madison smiled demurely back and sipped thoughtfully from her tall glass, her eyes fixed on his innocently carefree face as Allen sat back and basked in the admiring and envious glances coming from all sides.

Behind the scenes in the frantic hotel kitchens, Monsieur Ambroise, the *maître d'hôtel*, flitted anxiously among his subordinates, feeling rolls, sniffing sauces and tasting wines.

'Why is these breads in here and not out there?' he demanded, squeezing a crisp roll fastidiously. It exploded in a shower of brittle crumbs. He reached out and collared a young waiter with an earring and tight black trousers. 'Gary, why these butter is hard like the rock?' he complained, pinching the boy's taut buttock.

'Ya want it softer?' pouted the boy with heavy *double entendre*, swaggering away with a basket of fruit.

Ambroise's jaundiced eye lighted upon an unfamiliar figure dressed in scarlet-and-black waiter's livery who appeared either to be related to the Hunchback of Notre Dame or to be carrying something extremely bulky under his left arm. He was also wearing a surgical collar.

'Hey, Quasimodo,' he lisped, 'you have broken the arm?'

Walter Kornbluth grinned casually, peering through cracked spectacles. 'Not at all broken. It's just fractured in sixteen places,' he replied cheerfully.

Ambroise gave a French shrug – straight arms lifted slightly from the sides and then allowed to fall back. 'Why are you here?'

'Union sent me,' Walter bluffed.

At that moment, there was a fanfare from the banqueting hall.

'*Mon Dieu! Monsieur le Président est arrivé!*' gasped Ambroise. He snatched the plate of rolls and thrust them into Walter's hands. '*Allez . . . Allez vite . . .*' he commanded. 'These breads are late!'

Walter set off through the kitchen. 'The President's here . . . the President's here . . .' he chanted at the chefs and waiters.

As the staff sprang into even more frenzied action, Walter withdrew behind a partition and prepared his weaponry. Under the outsize waiter's jacket, two cylinders were strapped to his back and partly under his left arm, which was still held out at an angle by the surgical bracket. A short rubber hose connected to the cylinders and ending in a nozzled valve stuck out through the front of the jacket when Walter reached in and tugged it. Glancing round to make sure he was not observed, Walter kissed the nozzle for luck, directed it into a nearby sink and flicked the valve rapidly open and shut. A short but powerful jet of water squirted out. Walter kissed the nozzle again, tucked it out of sight and then checked his camera, nestling under his left arm beside the cylinders.

Taking a deep breath, he picked up the plate of bread rolls and edged his way through the milling throng of hotel staff towards the doors leading to the banqueting hall.

The tall, white-haired figure of the President of the United States accompanied by his squat, flouncily dressed First Lady moved with stately dignity towards the podium erected on a small stage at one end of the hall. All around them, clone-like secret service agents in crewcuts and characterless suits with shortwave radios in the breast-pockets, mingled impassively among the tables as the guests rose to their feet cheering, smiling and applauding enthusiastically.

Madison waved back energetically as the President waved with automaton vagueness at the sea of faces. She giggled delightedly as Allen winked at her as if to suggest that the great man had waved to her personally.

The President raised his hands modestly for silence and then leaned benevolently towards the bouquet of microphones in front of him.

'I'm just a corn-fed Kansas guy, but you people are the apple of my eye . . .' he boomed, stepping back to make way for the burst of wild cheers which greeted his hackneyed announcement. He stepped forward again. 'Thank you, my friends. Thank you so very, very much,' he drawled. 'Thank you, folks . . . I can't tell you just how great it is for me . . . for us to be back here in . . .' The President paused, as if searching for the word. There was a momentary awed and in some quarters apprehensive hush. 'Here in New York City . . .' he beamed at last, opening his arms expansively. The hall erupted in rapturous applause.

Unnoticed in the excitement and the euphoria, Kornbluth carried the dish of rolls awkwardly between the tables, the heavy cylinders and his broken arm causing him to walk with a kind of lopsided crouch. With a deferential grimace at the cheering guests, he plonked the rolls down on a table and then made his way hastily towards the table where Allen and Madison were hollaring and clapping with everyone else, smiling fondly at each other and then at the remote blue-suited figure on the distant podium.

Allen felt he wanted to race up to the microphones and announce to the President of the United States and the First Lady and all the dignitaries that he, Allen Bauer, was going to be married, married to the ravishing lady in the blue gown with the waist length straw-coloured hair . . .

Then one of the conspicuously anonymous secret servicemen ranged on the steps of the presidential podium suddenly caught sight of the bespectacled hunchback approaching through the loyal throng. Immediately he snatched out his radio. 'Alert, alert!' he snapped into it. 'Agent 5 intercept waiter with suspicious hump.'

At once an expressionless figure standing among the crowd near Allen and Madison's table moved swiftly towards Walter as he reached carefully into his bulging jacket for the nozzle.

'The guy's reaching for somethin'!' buzzed the first agent on the podium. 'All agents . . . Get him. Get him now.'

Agent 5 pushed his way up to Walter. 'Excuse me, sir, I'd like a word with you,' he muttered.

'About what?' retorted Kornbluth, his hand still inside his jacket.

'Just step this way, please.'

At that moment several more security agents surrounded him.

Walter shook his head irritably. 'Look this has got nothing to do with the President,' he protested vehemently.

But the ring of agents moved him irresistibly away from the podium and from Allen and Madison's table, and in the direction of the lobby, smiling reassuringly around them as though they were escorting a minor celebrity.

'This has nothing to do with the President . . .' Walter shouted as heads started turning.

The President paused in his address and watched the incident with calm detachment. 'Well, folks, I guess some guy just found out how much his dinner cost,' he quipped blandly, raising more sycophantic laughter and applause from all sides.

'I want to talk to the press,' Walter yelled in desperation. 'I have a formal statement to make on a matter of national significance.'

As Walter was bundled out to murmurs of 'Commie Democrat' and 'Red for Dead', the guests gradually sat down and the President resumed his speech. 'And in Bob Hollins you have a candidate for Congress who is in touch with the people . . .' he droned. 'Who built up a business that was once just a pushcart on wheels, a business left to him by his grandfather, which is today one of the largest factory concerns in the state . . .'

Allen was listening now. Somehow the President's words seemed relevant to himself, perhaps serving as a reproach to him for the way he had recently been neglecting Ralph Bauer

& Sons, Wholesale Produce.

Suddenly he became aware that Madison was whispering earnestly in his ear. 'Allen . . . Allen . . . It's time. It's time for me to tell you.'

He gaped at her, startled. 'What, now, honey? Now?'

'Yes, Allen. Right now.'

'OK, OK,' he grinned nervously. 'That's great.'

Madison shook her head emphatically. 'Not here, Allen.'

He glanced around and shrugged. 'Fine, fine. So let's go,' he proposed, rising and leading her towards the exit into the lobby.

As they threaded their way among the tables, the audience burst into sustained applause for the President's speech. Madison gazed around smiling in acknowledgement and waving graciously to left and right.

Under the awning at the hotel entrance Walter was noisily protesting to the crowd of security men hemming him against the wall.

'I am not crazy. I am not crazy!' he shouted. 'There is a mermaid in there with the President.'

'Sure.'

'I am a scientist and I am telling you . . .' Walter persisted as photographers and pressmen milled around the group.

'Where the hell's that goddamned car, for Christ's sake?' grunted a senior agent. 'We gotta get this Commie lunatic outta here fast.'

At that moment, Allen and Madison came out of the lobby and Allen handed his car-park coupon to an attendant. 'Grey BMW,' he said, including a dollar.

As the boy ran eagerly across to the carpark, Allen glanced over at the commotion on the sidewalk. 'There's that crazy guy again,' he laughed, nudging Madison to look. Then he looked more closely. 'Hey honey, I know that guy,' he murmured, staring at Walter. 'I saw him up at Cape Cod. He was crazy then, but I never thought he was any kind of . . .'

Suddenly Walter noticed them. He flung out his right arm, pointing triumphantly at Madison. '*There she is*!' he screamed in an almost demented falsetto. 'That's her . . . that's her . . .'

Allen slipped his arm protectively round Madison's shoulders. 'It's OK, sweetheart, it's OK,' he murmured reassuringly. 'He's just some kinda nutter.'

Madison began to tremble and her face had gone ashen. Allen held her closer and kissed her cheek. 'OK, honey, we'll be out of here in a few minutes and on our way to Maryland . . . and you can tell me everything you want,' he promised.

Madison stared at the shouting, gesticulating figure of Walter as the agents jostled around him, her eyes filled with a strange and profound suspicion.

Walter went quiet when he noticed the high-pressure water extinguisher-cylinders which the agents had confiscated lying a few feet away on the kerb. He also noticed that the agents were mostly concentrating on watching the gorgeous creature on Allen's arm at the other side of the entrance.

He waited for a moment and then launched a frantic breakout, butting and clubbing with his plaster cast. Reaching the cylinders he seized the hose and grappled with the valve mechanism attached to the nozzle.

'It's OK. He's just a crazy man,' Allen murmured, feeling Madison tense up as Walter directed the nozzle at her.

'No, no, no, no . . .' she stuttered over and over again, clinging to his sleeve.

'He's got a gun!' someone shouted, as the agents sprang forward.

A fierce jet of water suddenly shot across the sidewalk and sprayed all over Allen and Madison.

'Get the gun!'

'No . . . please, no . . .' screamed Madison, as the water soaked her from head to foot.

'Grab him! Grab him!'

As Allen tried to shield Madison, someone seized him and grappled him to the ground. Allen fought his burly attacker ruthlessly as they rolled up and down the red carpet. Then the agent realised his mistake and jumped up, leaving Allen dazed and confused.

Madison was thrown sideways into the gutter, where she lay screaming helplessly as the water poured relentlessly over her legs and the dress clung tightly to her shapely outline.

Agents were rushing from all sides, tripping over Madison and trampling over Allen. Walter was finally buried under a struggling heap of secret servicemen, one of whom snatched the nozzle from him and turned off the valve.

With his head ringing and his vision blurred with pain, Allen sat up on the carpet. 'What the hell is going on here?' he yelled, at the top of his lungs.

As the agents sorted themselves out around him, Walter raised his head and stared at Madison. 'There . . . there, I was right . . . I was right!' he screamed, pointing at her.

The agents looked round and were abruptly speechless.

Allen stared at the sobbing figure lying drenched in the gutter. The hair on the nape of his neck began to prickle and stir like the quills on a porcupine. His mouth fell open and his face froze.

From beneath the hem of Madison's sodden dress a slim, glittering tail lay over the kerbstone, its pearly scales flickering with myriad colours and delicate shades of iridescent light. The double scimitar of its fin lay gently stirring in the puddle of water.

'Behold. The mermaid!' Walter Kornbluth cried, delirious with success.

Pandemonium broke out again. Television and press personnel surged around Madison, trampling over Allen in their eagerness to get the first pictures and interviews. Kornbluth pushed through the stunned secret servicemen, his eyes ablaze with triumph, muttering 'I was right . . . I was right . . .' like some magical incantation.

Allen sat in paralysed isolation, gaping at Madison, numbed with horror and shock.

'Who are you? Where do you come from? What is your name? Who brought you here?' The reporters' barrage of questions ran off Madison like the water still trickling down her face. She gazed at Allen through her tears, while the flashbulbs exploded cruelly in her brimming eyes.

'Hey, Miss... look this way, please... turn your head to me... smile please, Miss... Get her hair outta the way... let's see the tits... Pull the dress up higher... Get the goddam dress off her...'

Eventually Allen got shakily to his feet and stood staring down at her like the rest of the rapidly swelling crowd.

Slowly Madison stretched out her hand towards him. 'Allen... Allen...' she pleaded. 'Please, Allen...'

But he just stood there among the gawping, pointing, chattering crowd.

'Grab her,' shouted a senior agent. 'Grab him. Grab everybody!'

Agents converged on Kornbluth, and Allen was taken and held by two men.

'Let's pick her up,' ordered the senior agent, leading a number of agents over to Madison.

'Allen...' she moaned piteously, her gleaming fin twitching spasmodically under the glare of the TV lights and the popping flashbulbs.

Still Allen stared silently down at her, rigid with shock and unable to speak. His eyes were filled with a mixture of disbelief, horror and sadness.

The agents picked the strange creature up from the gutter and carried her unceremoniously through the jostling, babbling onlookers and the horde of ruthless media vultures to an enormous black Cadillac limousine with smoked-glass windows that had just whispered up to the entrance.

Allen watched blankly as his lady from the sea was bundled hastily into the car and it cruised swiftly away, followed by a stream of photographers and video crews running in pursuit in the hope of a last picture. Then he too was hustled away into a second limousine and driven off.

Last to go was Walter Kornbluth. Swelling with importance, he kept shouting that he was very happy to be interviewed and would pose for photographs. But by the time the press people noticed him again it was too late. He too was marched to a black Cadillac and driven quickly away.

18

At noon the following day, Dr Ronald Ross, Curator of Palaeontology, walked briskly along the basement corridor of the Museum of Natural History dressed in a white laboratory coat and sporting a red bow-tie. He brusquely greeted the handful of FBI personnel hanging around the corridor leading to the Research Department, tapped his identity badge and strode officiously along to the laboratory buried in the bowels of the huge building. He nodded curtly to Sergeant Buckhalter of the US Marines, who stood on guard at the door, sten gun at the ready.

'Afternoon, sir,' Buckhalter rapped out, snapping to attention.

Ross paused and smiled, touched by this demonstration of respect for his authority. 'Buckhalter,' he acknowledged crisply and entered the laboratory like a classical actor making an entrance onto the stage.

A functional metal staircase led down into a large chamber on two levels. The upper level consisted of a dimly lit mezzanine section containing monitoring and computer equipment. In the subdued light, white-coated figures pored over video screens and the displays and print-outs from metabolic testing equipment. On the lower level, a huge glass tank about ten feet square and filled with water stood in the centre of the chamber. Above it, a steel gantry supported powerful lights and hoisting apparatus. The chamber was silent except for the chatter of teleprinters and the bleeping of oscilloscopes.

*

Ross strode into the monitoring area. 'Anything gentlemen?' he asked hopefully. 'Mr Fujimoto?'

A serious young Japanese looked up from his keyboard terminal and shook his head. 'Nothing, Dr Ross. No change.'

Ross glanced round at the others. All shook their heads and returned to their work. He beckoned Fujimoto to follow and descended to the lower floor. They went over to the tank and looked in.

Allen was standing naked in a corner of the tank with the water up to his neck. Attached to various points on his body were thin wires sprouting from a kind of belt round his waist. A cable led from the belt up along the gantry and divided again into connections to the various devices in the monitoring area.

Allen stared back at Ross and Fujimoto with frightened, bewildered eyes. 'Listen . . . I am a man. I am not a fish . . .' he murmured, as if for the millionth time, in a hoarse and weary voice. 'How many times do I have to tell you guys? Now will you just let me out of here, please?'

Ross stared at Allen with cold scientific detachment, appraising the young virile body with steely grey eyes. Then he turned to Fujimoto. 'Let's try some interaction,' he suggested impassively.

His colleague nodded eagerly. 'Fine,' he agreed. He signalled to a technician standing beside a large crate beneath the hoist. 'Put her in Jim.'

In the crate, Madison was lying like a beached dolphin, trussed in a kind of harness attached to the hoisting gear. Like Allen, she wore a belt round her waist with electrodes leading to different parts of her body and a cable connecting her to the monitoring apparatus. The scales of her fin and tail were dulled and chafed and she was panting under the shroud of wet blankets and the hot lights.

The technician removed the blankets and operated the hoist. Madison was lifted out of the crate, swung out over the tank and lowered slowly into the water. While this was being done with clinical efficiency, Allen closed his eyes and averted his face. The harness was released and hauled back out of the water and Madison began to swim around the bottom of the tank, her tail and fin undulating slowly and gracefully up and down. Ross and Fujimoto watched intently through the glass, while the technicians concentrated on their scanners and monitors.

Madison swam to and fro a few times, her body regaining a little of its tone and lustre once more. Gradually she swam up to the surface and along beside Allen, her hair a glorious golden cloud in the water brushing against his legs and hips. Allen held his face away from her like a statue.

Madison murmured his name like a magic spell, but he did not respond. 'I guess they thought you might be one of us . . .' she whispered faintly.

There was a pause. 'Yeah. I guess . . .' Allen said at last almost inaudibly, still looking firmly away from her.

Madison laid her hands gently on his chest. 'You said that whatever my secret was you would understand . . .' she reminded him earnestly.

At last Allen turned to look at her, his face twisted with anguish. 'Yeah, I know . . . I know, but I . . . I . . .' he stammered, lapsing helplessly into silence and looking away again.

'You thought at least I was a human being.'

Allen nodded briefly.

Madison reached out to touch his face, but Allen lurched away from her, sending violent ripples round the edge of the tank.

Dodging the splashes, Ross and Fujimoto peered through the glass, growing restless with frustration and disappointment. Ross took off his spectacles, polished them irritably on the hem of his laboratory coat and replaced them on his small sharp nose.

Madison murmured Allen's name a few more times, but he did not even look at her. Then she turned sadly and dived to the bottom of the tank and lay there motionless, her hair floating over her like an exotic weed.

Ross turned abruptly on his heel and clattered up the

staircase to the monitoring area, where his team were still hopefully scanning their instruments for some sign of unusual activity. 'He's been in that goddam water for twelve hours. He's obviously just a man,' Ross growled resentfully. 'Get Tarzan outta there and concentrate on the . . . on her.'

While the technicians hauled Allen out of the tank, Madison curved herself over until her head rested on her fin and lay perfectly still, isolated and defeated under the cold glare of the lights.

Half an hour later, a transit van with darkened windows drew up at the entrance to Allen's apartment block. As the side-door slid open, a crowd of photographers and journalists surged round it pushing and shoving shamelessly. Two FBI agents got out with Allen between them. One of them quickly removed the blindfold round Allen's eyes and then the two agents jumped back into the van and it drove rapidly away.

Allen stood on the kerb blinking in the early afternoon sunlight and the glare of sizzling flashbulbs and television lights as the fusillade of questions erupted.

'Greg Martin, WMET Radio here with Alan Bauer . . .' rapped a pushy young man flourishing a microphone. 'Mr Bauer, just when and where did you first meet the mermaid?'

Allen tried to force his way across the sidewalk, but his path to the door was solidly blocked. 'Ah look, sorry folks, but I don't want to . . .' he mumbled ineffectually, waving his hands.

'Mr Bauer, tell me, where did you meet?' asked a girl from one of the women's magazines. 'How long have you known each other?'

Allen shook his head, vainly trying to push the notebooks, lenses and microphones aside.

'Did you know she was a mermaid?'

'Did you actually make love to her, Allen?' someone shouted from the back.

'Oh, now that's . . . that's a stupid question,' Allen snapped, fighting his way towards the revolving door.

'Is it true that she eats worms? Actually eats them?'

'Mr Bauer, did you have to make love to her under water?'

Allen swung round furiously. 'Now listen, Jack, that's none of your goddam business,' he hissed ominously.

'Hey, Mr Bauer, is she some kinda mutant from the effects of effluent pollution?' demanded a spotty boy from an ecology magazine.

'Yeah, is it possible she's some kind of missing link?'

'You're the one with the missing link,' Allen snapped back, managing to almost reach the door where Tim was struggling to clear a path for him.

A smartly dressed middle-aged woman in a tight trouser-suit grabbed Allen's sleeve. 'I'm from *People Magazine*, Mr Bauer. Is it true that she's also seeing Burt Reynolds?'

Allen turned back to face the voracious mob. 'Oh, for Christ's sake . . .' he screamed.

At that moment Freddie Bauer drove up in his red Porsche. He was wearing a classy sheepskin coat with a checked trilby perched jauntily on his small head. With surprising agility he leaped out over the door and started clearing a swathe through the throng like a harvester in a wheatfield.

'Leave the guy alone!' he yelled. 'Leave my little brother alone. Get the hell outta the way here.'

Allen's drawn, greyish face opened up in a blooming smile of deliverance. 'Please, let me through. Freddie, get me out of here,' he pleaded, battling his way towards his huge brother.

Freddie reached him and seized him in a gigantic embrace. 'You OK, Allen?' he murmured.

'Yeah. I just . . . just get me out of here.'

Freddie surveyed the jostling media with a frown of jaundiced expertise. 'Is anyone here from *Penthouse* magazine?' he boomed, in a foghorn voice.

There were catcalls of derision and shouts of denial from the mob.

'Then we ain't talkin'!' Freddie blasted contemptuously, towing Allen swiftly along the sidewalk and lifting him bodily into the car. And with his plump fist hard on the horn, Freddie accelerated away leaving the frustrated bunch still shouting questions, while Tim adjusted his braided cap with professional disdain.

Down at the wharf, an uncanny hush fell over the produce market as Freddie drove Allen up to the warehouse. As they walked through the open-fronted store, people stopped work and stood gazing at Allen with awed curiosity. On the stairs leading up to the office, Freddie stopped and looked disdainfully down at them.

'What the hell you all gawpin' at?' he demanded. 'You never saw a guy who slept with a fish before? Come on, you guys, get back to work!' he chivvied them, with a stream of Sergeant Bilko growls of encouragement.

In the office, Mrs Stimler sat placidly crocheting a tea-cosy, the plastic bath-hat jammed tightly over her froth of grey curls.

'Oh Mr Bauer, you had a million messages . . .' she crowed, picking up a mass of small pieces of scrap paper. 'And you got calls from CBS, NBC, ABC, AP, UPI . . .'

Scarcely hearing her, Allen grabbed the newspaper off the dusty typewriter. Its banner headline read: MERMAID FOUND AT FUND-RAISING. HELD BY FEDS. His exhausted eyes scanned the closely printed columns of the item without taking anything in at all.

'. . . Ted Turner, *Time* magazine, *Joe Franklyn Show*, *Marineland*, Ripley's *Believe it or Not* . . . and Mrs Paul,' concluded Mrs Stimler panting with breathless excitement and scattering the bits of paper like confetti all over her desk and into the various paper cups of cold coffee she had accumulated.

Freddie smiled and nodded patiently. 'Thank you, but not now Mrs Stimler, not now.'

He drew Allen into the inner office.

'Fishman . . .' Allen whispered, staring at the newspaper in his white-knuckled hands. 'Fishman?' He flung the paper savagely at the wall and sank weakly onto the couch Freddie had installed.

Freddie nodded. 'Yeah, that's what they're calling you on TV too,' he grinned, retrieving the paper and studying it proudly. 'Personally I think it's kinda cute,' he chuckled.

Allen stared silently at the contented fish goggling at him from the bubbling aquarium in the corner.

'Well, how is she?' asked Freddie brightly.

Allen shrugged. 'How is she? She's a mermaid,' he answered impassively, still gazing at the brilliant fish.

Freddie took off his sheepskin coat and squeezed himself into a smartly tailored sports jacket.

'I just don't understand it,' Allen muttered after a pause. 'All my life . . . all my goddam life I've been waiting, waiting for someone. And now when I finally find her . . . she's a fish!'

'Nobody said love's perfect,' Freddie pointed out complacently.

Allen stood up and wandered round the office as though he had never seen it before. 'Freddie, I don't expect it to be perfect. But for God's sake . . . it's usually human.' He thrust his hands into his pockets and laughed with scornful irony. 'I mean, everyday people meet and they fall in love. Every day. And just look at what I got . . .'

He sat down on the couch again and sank his head in his hands.

Freddie rounded on him, suddenly angry. 'Just look at what you got. Yeah, let's take a good look at what you got,' he said vehemently. 'People fall in love every day – is that what you said?'

'Yeah.'

'Well that's just bullshit. It doesn't work that way,' Freddie told him firmly. 'Look, do you remember how happy you were with her? That is, of course, when you weren't busy drivin' yourself crazy worryin'. Do you realise how happy you were?' Freddie wandered round the office shaking his head and twisting his hands together as he tried to find the words he wanted.

Then he sat down on the arm of the couch and leaned over Allen. 'People fall in love every day? Come on, Allen, some people will *never* be that happy,' he protested. 'I'll never be that happy. Never.'

Freddie paused. Allen looked up at him blankly, without any sign of response.

Freddie stood up decisively. 'What the hell am I tryin' to talk to you for?' he exploded, making for the door. 'You don't know nothin' at all. Nothing.'

And he went out to consult Mrs Stimler, while Allen remained hunched on the couch in the shafts of pale sunshine from the blinds, his head in his hands. Meanwhile the fish had crowded to the front of the aquarium and were watching him with wide-open, enigmatic eyes.

19

Walter Kornbluth looked on unhappily as Madison was tipped back into the tank for the second time that afternoon, while Dr Ross and the others studied their instruments carefully. Madison sank listlessly to the bottom of the tank, making no attempt to swim at all. Walter stared at the colourless, dull scales of her fin and tail with mounting concern. The brilliant pearly sheen had gone. Many of the scales had broken off and were floating eerily up to the surface like brown leaves on a dirty pond. The creature's skin was greyish and waxy, no longer firm and gleaming bronze. Her eyes were lifeless and fixed unseeingly on him. Her hair was matted and coarse and it clung in rope-like strands. Her breasts had begun to sag and had lost their former ripe fullness.

Kornbluth turned to the white-coated team on the mezzanine. 'Hey, doesn't she look a little pale?' he suggested mildly.

Everyone ignored him. Ross tore a length of print-out from a computer terminal and peered at the endless wavy traces and smudges.

'Good. That's a very good day's work,' he announced in his thin nasal whine. 'Now tomorrow I want to see how she interacts with other marine life – fish, lobsters, turtles, rays, octopuses, squid, echinoderms . . . the whole works.'

Mr Fujimoto nodded enthusiastically. 'OK, Dr Ross, I'll fix it all up for the morning.'

Ross gathered up papers, graphs and tapes and stuffed them into his briefcase. 'Fine. And after that we should be about ready for the comprehensive internal examination.'

Walter ran across the chamber to the foot of the stairs, his eyes popping incredulously. 'Internal examination?' he shouted.

Ross looked down at the intruder with undisguised contempt. 'Naturally,' he whined. 'I shall want to investigate her pulmonary system, her neurological functions, her reproductive organs . . . everything.' He turned abruptly and started up the stairs towards the exit.

Walter glared up at him through the metal grille of the mezzanine landing. 'Dr Ross, are we considering how the specimen is reacting to the investigation procedure itself?' he enquired, wincing as the surgical collar he was wearing dug into his neck as he craned upward.

The Curator of Palaeontology paused and squinted sneeringly through the grating. '*I* am considering everything, Kornbluth,' he declared with withering finality.

Walter gestured towards the forlorn and motionless figure at the bottom of the tank. 'Oh, I'm sure you are, Dr Ross,' he shouted. 'But are you considering this? Are you considering the possibility that you might be behaving like a sadistic pig?'

There was a chilling silence. Then Ross bent down and peered through the landing at the insolent nonentity beneath his feet. 'While we are bearing our souls, Mr Kornbluth,' he snarled, his grey dentures foaming with hatred, 'I must honestly tell you that I have never considered you to be a man of science.' Ross stood up again, gesturing dramatically around the chamber. 'You are not a member of my team,' he reminded him spitefully.

Walter glanced jealously at the sniggering researchers working on the mezzanine above him.

'So why don't you run along now, Walter? Run along and see if you can find us a unicorn?' With that parting shot, Ross clattered up the last few steps and strode out of the laboratory.

Stung to the heart by Ross's dismissive taunts, Walter walked back slowly to the tank. He took off his cracked glasses and gazed pityingly at the lifeless creature on the bottom. Her face was still turned towards him, her eyes expressionless and dead. A lump came into Walter's throat and the pain in his arm and his neck and his broken teeth was eclipsed by the silent agony of the helpless mermaid through the glass. The enormity of her cruel plight combined with the Curator's arrogant smugness to fire a flame of dark resolution in Walter's innermost being. Crippled, ridiculed and unacknowledged, he resolved to wreak a terrible revenge on his tormentors and detractors.

Turning on his heel, he stalked out of the laboratory, his eyes gleaming with malevolent purpose. But half-way along the basement corridor of the museum he suddenly slowed down, seemingly less determined that before. He had just remembered that he had a very unpleasant appointment the following morning.

Allen sat slumped in a chair in his apartment, listening to the endless mocking trickle of the fountain and trying not to look at the inviting smile of the mermaid on her rock. All night his mind had been whirling round and round in a relentless succession of images and memories, some starkly vivid, others confused and blurred. Yesterday he had felt numbed and cold about the whole thing, but now he gradually felt his blood rising in a surging desire for some kind of revenge. He was filled with a need to smash and destroy. Yet behind these feelings there was a deep and enduring longing of which he was only vaguely conscious and its irresistible force only served to strengthen his instinct for vengeance.

As dawn broke, he jumped up, threw on a jacket and hurried out to get his car from the basement garage.

Walter Kornbluth sat rigidly in the dentist's chair warily eyeing all the gadgetry of sadistic torture surrounding him. He was feeling in a masochistic mood and it seemed a fitting place to be after all. The surgery was equipped with all the aids to promote relaxation and to banish fear – subdued lighting, soothing muzak, indoor cacti and a tankful of fish under the window – but Kornbluth was resolved to suffer and the fish spurred him on even more.

'What's that?' he gasped, as the dentist approached with a large, loaded hypodermic syringe.

'Why, it's painkiller, Mr Kornbluth,' the dentist lisped. 'Whoever punched you in the mouth cracked your tooth and we are going to be very, very close to that nerve this morning.'

Walter shook his head firmly. 'Listen, I don't deserve any painkiller. Just drill.'

The dentist looked at his patient strangely and then put down the syringe on the tray and picked up the drill. Walter's head and left arm were already held rigid by the brace and the plaster and now the rest of his scrawny body locked in rigor mortis.

'Oh, well, if you want pain we certainly strive to please,' sighed the dentist, inserting the gleaming drill into Walter's gaping mouth. 'Hold on, here we go.'

Walter closed his eyes and thought of sea-scorpions.

At that precise moment the door from the waiting-room burst open and Allen Bauer rushed into the surgery. The drill buzzed around Walter's mouth in a rasping zigzag as the startled dentist spun round.

'What the hell are you doing in here?' he shouted.

Allen was poised like a panther about to spring on its prey and sink its teeth into living flesh. 'Just get outta here . . .' he snarled.

'OK, OK, OK . . .' The dentist dropped the drill, which rattled horribly around in Walter's ravaged mouth, and ran out of the surgery slamming the door behind him.

With agonised gutteral cries Walter spat the fizzing drill out of his mouth and leaped from the chair, backing away from the menacing intruder.

'Let's you and me talk,' Allen suggested, stepping forward.

Walter lurched sideways and snatched the hypodermic from the tray, flourishing it defensively. 'Just you stay away from me,' he whispered hoarsely.

Allen backed off a little. 'Hey, put that thing down,' he muttered.

Walter took a couple of steps towards him, grimacing fiendishly.

'I said let's just talk,' Allen protested, attempting a conciliatory grin. 'Come on, now, put that needle down.'

'Stay away from me . . . you're crazy,' Kornbluth retorted, making vicious stabbing gestures with the syringe.

Allen cautiously backed round the chair as Walter advanced on him. Then he suddenly raced round and grabbed Walter from behind in a powerful bearhug. 'Put it down!' he yelled in Walter's ear.

With a sudden bloodcurdling shriek, like some karate enthusiast, Walter stabbed down at Allen's thigh. But the needle shot into his own leg and the war-cry changed into a frenzied yelp of pain and shock as the plunger of the syringe was pushed down and the anaesthetic injected.

Walter collapsed into the chair moaning. 'What a week I'm having!' he whimpered, rubbing his sore thigh.

Allen paced round and round the immobilised patient, finding it really difficult to express the maelstrom of feelings inside him. 'You've . . . you've ruined my . . . you've destroyed my life, Kornbluth,' he blurted out after a pause, waving the empty hypodermic he had taken from his agonised victim.

'But I didn't mean to,' Walter protested pathetically. 'I just had to prove to everyone that I wasn't crazy. That I was right.'

Allen ranged around, seething and silent.

'I'm a man of science,' Walter continued doggedly. 'I just didn't think about how it would affect you or . . . or her.' He tried vainly to massage the feeling back into his numb leg. 'But listen, Bauer, I'm really a really nice guy, you know. If I had friends, you could ask them,' he claimed desperately.

Allen angrily gesticulated with the syringe in Walter's miserable face. 'I've been on the phone to every goddam employee of the United States Government calling them sons of bitches,' he raged. 'Nobody can even get in there to see her, wherever she is.'

Walter stopped rubbing his senseless leg and thought very

quickly. He gave Allen a sly sidelong glance. 'I can. I can get to see her any time,' he declared casually.

Allen stopped in his tracks and stared at Kornbluth for several seconds with narrowed eyes. Then he flung down the syring, grabbed Walter's lapels and lifted him bodily out of the chair. 'Come on, then. Come on. What the hell are we waiting for?' he yelled, propelling Walter towards the door.

They burst through the waiting-room in front of the open-mouthed dentist, receptionist and patients like a tornado. Walter hopped along like a one-legged mantis, his right leg dangling uselessly around at the end of his crooked body, frantically trying to keep up with Allen's sprinting stride. 'What a week I'm having . . .' he cried, as he was bundled down the stairs and out into the street to Allen's waiting car.

20

An hour later, his right leg now functioning again, and ignoring the pain in his tooth, his arm and his neck, Walter Kornbluth led Allen and Freddie into the Musuem of Natural History and down into the basement. The Bauer brothers were both wearing white laboratory coats over their clothes, just like Walter. The trio walked along with a brisk businesslike air, exchanging the occasional nervous glance and grin of encouragement as they reached the corridor leading to the Research Department.

Turning the corner, they were stopped by young Lieutenant Ingram of the US Marines. He rose smartly from his desk, hurriedly closing the Danish health and fitness magazine he had been studying, with its photographs of enormous teenage bodybuilders doing extraordinary things with bronzed Scandinavian goddesses.

'Good afternoon, Dr Kornbluth. I was not expecting you back today,' he said, with a toothpaste commercial smile.

Walter tried to look relaxed despite the neck brace and the permanently akimbo left arm. He gestured to Allen and Freddie. 'These gentlemen are Dr Jarred and Dr Johanssen from the Stockholm Institute,' he said casually.

Lieutenant Ingram consulted his clipboard and frowned. 'I thought they were coming in later with Dr Ross,' he replied. 'There's nobody in the laboratory at the moment.'

Walter smothered his sigh of relief with a hearty laugh, waving his hand airily. 'Oh no, no, no, that story was just cooked up to fool the press,' he explained.

Ingram nodded and flashed his piercing blue eyes and

smiled his toothpaste smile again. He turned to the two strangers. 'Well, gentlemen I'm actually half Swedish myself!' he informed them, eyeing Allen's handsome face and wiry supple physique with obvious appreciation.

Next moment Allen and Freddie froze and their mouths dropped open in astonishment as Ingram uttered a couple of amiable sentences in fluent Swedish. Walter looked as though he wanted to sink through the floor, but Allen and Freddie quickly pulled themselves together and nodded enthusiastically at the lieutenant.

'Ah. Yah. Hey. Yah,' said Allen.

'Oh. Hey. Yah. Hey,' said Freddie in total agreement.

One after the other they seized Ingram's hand and pumped it energetically up and down.

'Sure,' Freddie added.

'Yeah. Sure,' Allen agreed.

Walter joined in with a few more 'Yahs' and 'Heys' for good measure and then motioned Allen and Freddie to proceed down the corridor to the laboratory.

But Ingram stopped them. 'Just a second,' he said and proceeded to deliver several complex sentences, again in perfect Swedish. Walter's face warped into a look of panic-stricken dismay while Allen smiled and nodded at Ingram as if he could somehow hypnotise the young marine or make him just disappear.

Then Freddie suddenly came out with a short sentence in a solemn singsong voice that certainly sounded like authentic Swedish.

There was an agonising pause. Then Ingram stared wide-eyed at the vast figure and clapped him several times on the back while roaring with hearty laughter. Allen and Walter joined in hesitantly, having not the remotest idea what Freddie had said. Ingram waved them past the checkpoint, still laughing and slapping Freddie on the back like an old mess buddy. He watched them disappear down the corridor and then sat down at his desk and started leafing eagerly through the magazine as though he were looking for something.

'How the hell did you do that?' Allen demanded out of the side of his mouth as they approached Sergeant Buckhalter at his post outside the door to the laboratory at the far end of the long corridor.

Freddie beamed smugly. 'Well, just let me tell you something,' he confided. 'Many of your finer quality nudie blue films come from Sweden. Well, after you've seen them four or five hundred times the stuff starts to sink in.'

'What the hell did you say to the guy then?' Allen asked, still incredulous.

Freddie drew Allen's and Walter's heads closer to his own. 'I just told the guy I had a twelve-inch prick,' he sniggered.

Walter looked shocked, but Allen hugged Freddie gleefully and kissed him on both cheeks.

Sergeant Buckhalter's stern face under his squat helmet and his loaded sten gun at the ready reminded them of the serious nature of their mission.

Walter strode nonchalantly up to him. 'Morning, Buckhalter,' he cried.

The short little Sergeant frowned apologetically. 'I'm real sorry, Dr Kornbluth, but I'm not supposed to let anybody in there until Dr Ross gets here with them Swedes,' he declared adamantly.

Walter jerked his thumb at the Bauer brothers. 'These are the two Swedish gentlemen,' he informed him.

Buckhalter gazed at Allen and Freddie sceptically. 'These are Swedes?' he exclaimed. He pointed his sten gun at Allen. 'Isn't that one there kinda dark?'

Kornbluth smiled patiently and pushed his glasses up his big nose. 'Dr Jarred is a little soiled from the long journey,' he explained carefully. 'Come on now, Buckhalter, we have work to do. Let us in there.'

The Sergeant shook his head unhappily. 'No, I'm real sorry, sir, but I'm not supposed . . .'

'What are you afraid of?' Walter demanded with a forced laugh. 'Do you think we are going to steal the mermaid or something?'

Freddie thumped Allen between the shoulder blades. 'Stealing the mermaid... stealing the mermaid...' he bellowed in a fake accent.

Allen laughed faintly.

'What am I gonna do?' Walter protested, appealing to the Sergeant's common sense. 'Fold her in half and stick her in a briefcase or something?'

Freddie thumped Allen again, causing him to cough and blink his watering eyes. 'In the briefing case. In a half!' he roared.

Allen smiled wanly, wishing to hell they'd never got themselves into such a ludicrous situation.

Buckhalter squirmed in confusion and embarrassment. 'Oh well, I guess it'll be okay,' he mumbled shamefacedly, turning and opening the door for them. 'Yeah, OK, go right ahead, gentlemen.'

Walter led the way, tense and apprehensive. As Freddie passed he poked Buckhalter's tin hat. 'Good joke in there,' he grinned.

The Sergeant's face smiled, but his eyes remained dead serious. 'Yeah,' he muttered.

Allen shut the door firmly behind them.

The laboratory was dark and deserted. Here and there the scattered pilot lights and flickering oscilloscopes and the quiet clicking of the equipment provided the only signs of life. Walter switched on the overhead lights and Freddie gazed in childlike wonder at the mysterious and motionless figure curved into a foetal bundle at the bottom of the tank, her hair covering her modestly like a shawl.

Alarmed at her stillness, Allen ran down the staircase followed closely by Walter, who hurried across to the monitoring equipment.

'Hell, is she OK?' Walter cried, as Allen clambered up onto the gantry and ruffled the murky water with his hands. Allen shook his head uncertainly, murmuring Madison's name under his breath.

Very slowly Madison uncurled like an opening flower and looked up at him through the water. Allen smiled down at her tenderly. She seemed not to recognise him for a moment. Then she gave him a brief little smile. Freddie watched from the staircase with tears in his eyes as the creature flicked her tail gently and glided gracefully up to the surface. As her face emerged from the water Allen bent down, took it in his hands and kissed her cheeks, her nose, her eyes and finally, with passionate gentleness, her mouth.

At once there was a flurry of flashing lights and quickening pulses and pings from the equipment, as Madison began to respond to Allen's kiss with hungry lips. Walter watched in amazement as pens whizzed off the edges of graphs and traces whipped off the oscilloscope screens. Print-outs started chattering furiously and disgorging yards and yards of closely printed data.

'Hi,' Allen whispered, cradling Madison's head against his chest.

She was silent for a while, as if she could not believe that she was not dreaming. 'Hi,' she murmured eventually.

Freddie clapped his hands with rapture and slowly descended the stairs like a father on his daughter's wedding day.

Allen let the happy tears drip off his chin into the water. 'So this is the great dark secret you've been keeping from me,' he smiled. 'Is it just that you're a mermaid, or is there something else?'

'No, Allen. That's all. Now you know everything,' Madison whispered wistfully, clasping her arms around his neck. 'Allen, don't feel guilty,' she pleaded, kissing his ear.

'Guilty? Guilty about what?'

'About not loving me any more.'

Allen reached into the water and drew her up to him, embracing her glistening body and nestling his face against hers. 'Oh, Madison,' he murmured, 'all the time we were together you always knew what I was feeling. Can't you tell now, sweetheart?'

There was a long pause. Then Madison kissed his curly

dark hair and drew his face into her breasts. 'Yes, Allen, I can tell now,' she smiled, her eyes brightening again and her body growing firmer with some of her former vibrancy returning as they held each other close.

'OK, you guys!' Walter called out, trying to restore a little discipline into the proceedings. He rapidly outlined their next move.

Freddie wiped away his tears and took off his vast laboratory coat before clambering up onto the gantry to help Allen pull Madison out of the tank. Then they quickly wrapped her in the coat, like a corpse in a shroud, and carried her up the staircase.

Outside in the deserted corridor, Hiram Buckhalter was singing to help counter the boredom of his lonely vigil. 'Well, left my wife in New Orleans . . . Forty-eight kids and a can of beans . . .'

All at once the door to the laboratory flew open and Kornbluth staggered out, glasses awry, tie under one ear and white coat in tatters. 'Oh, my God . . . oh, my God!' he screamed, gaping in terror at the sergeant.

Buckhalter looked around in all directions, nearly flooring Walter with his flailing machine-gun. 'What the hell . . . ?' he gulped, choking as his loose helmet strap flapped into his mouth.

Walter pushed him away from the door. 'Stand back man!' he shouted. 'Keep away.' He dived back into the laboratory. 'Oh, my God. Cover his face for chrissake!' he yelled, out of sight.

'What's happened? What's goin' on in there?' Buckhalter mumbled, aiming his sten gun at the door.

The door opened again. 'Keep back!' Walter warned as he and Allen manhandled the shrouded body into the corridor.

Allen stared at the sergeant in horror. 'That creature . . . that thing . . .' he gasped. 'Dr Johanssen just bent down to examine her and . . . and suddenly these kinda rays . . . these rays came out of her eyes.'

Walter shuddered and nodded, doing his best to support his share of the bundle with his one serviceable arm. 'Horrible. It was horrible,' he croaked.

Swallowing hard, Buckhalter stepped towards the door, pointing his gun uncertainly in front of him.

'No. Don't go in there!' Allen screamed, kicking the door shut behind him. 'She'll... she'll melt your face right off . . .'

Buckhalter hesitated, fiddling with his flapping helmet strap. 'I knew it. I just knew somethin' like this was goin' to happen . . .' he bleated, his pasty face suddenly red with panic. 'What shall I do? What shall I do?'

'Oh, stop whining,' Walter snapped recklessly, straightening his glasses. 'Seal off the entire area immediately.'

Buckhalter turned to the wall-phone trembling all over. 'That's it! That's it! I'll call the Pentagon.'

Walter heaved himself closer to the sergeant. 'Pentagon? Are you crazy?' he threatened. 'Do you want to be responsible for causing a national panic?'

'I don't want to die . . .' whimpered the sweating sergeant.

Letting go of Madison's tail, Walter slapped Buckhalter hard. 'Pull yourself together, man,' he ordered harshly. 'The time has come for you to take a hold on the situation.' He picked up his end of the bundle again.

Buckhalter suddenly pointed at the bundle in suspicious astonishment. 'But that Dr Johanssen, he was . . .' He spread his hands wide apart like a bragging angler in the clubhouse.

Walter glanced at Allen in alarm.

'Oh, those rays they shrank him up like a potato chip,' he explained hastily with a macabre grimace.

Kornbluth stared sternly at the bewildered sergeant. 'Now listen Buckhalter, I don't want you to let anybody, not *anybody* into that laboratory,' he commanded. 'I shall be back. I shall be back with . . . with nuclear weapons . . . Come on, Dr Jarred.'

Buckhalter watched impotently as the two white-coated figures hurried away along the corridor with their terrible burden. Then he set his jaw, gripped his gun, drew himself upright and . . . and to his disgust realised that in all the panic, something quite irregular had occurred in his trousers.

21

Like undercover agents on a life-and-death mission far inside enemy territory, Allen and Walter Kornbluth manhandled the long, white mummy-like bundle down the front steps of the Museum of Natural History and sat it upright in the passenger seat of Allen's BMW. Allen jumped in beside it and Walter manoeuvred himself awkwardly into the back. As Allen tried to reverse out of the cramped parking space, Madison shook her head free from the tight fold of Freddie's laboratory coat and started kissing him passionately on the mouth.

'Yeah . . . later. Later, please, sweetheart,' Allen protested, doing his best to fend her off and skidding out into the busy traffic stream with suicidal abandon.

Jammed in the back, Walter kept watch for pursuers through the rear window. Madison unbuttoned Allen's shirt with feverish fingers and started kissing and caressing his chest and stomach. Allen stared through the windscreen, struggling to concentrate as he accelerated recklessly through the congested streets, weaving in and out and shrugging his shoulders whenever they slipped through a perilously narrow gap. Occasionally Allen yielded to Madison's persuasive lips while Walter yelled frantic warnings about the traffic situation on all sides. Then Madison thrust the laboratory coat aside, revealing her long, slim legs. Allen glanced down and smiled and put his right hand on her thigh, moving it slowly up and down as he swung the steering wheel crazily from side to side with his left.

They had only been going a few minutes when they were

forced to stop and queue at an intersection snarl-up.

Walter leaned over the seat grinning with boyish glee. 'Want to know something? I don't think we're being followed,' he announced.

Allen laughed. 'But... but this is all just too easy...' he said, exploring Madison's thigh with shameless thoroughness.

Walter pulled the laboratory coat a little more modestly around Madison's naked shoulders in order to conceal her proudly swinging breasts from the other drivers in the jam.

'We did it and it was all my idea!' he whooped deliriously.

'Walter, you're a genius!' Allen agreed, grinning at Kornbluth's wild reflection in the rearview mirror.

'I admit it!' Walter laughed. 'But the Swedish thing was brilliant. That was your idea.'

'Well, yeah. I admit it.'

'A real classy touch.' Walter enthused.

'I didn't even like you when I first met you,' Allen confessed, continuing to caress Madison's thigh while she murmured with pleasure. 'In fact, I hated your guts!'

Walter shrieked with laughter. 'Funny, but nobody likes me when they first meet me,' he boasted.

Allen felt under the coat and among Madison's tumbling hair and cupped her breast in one hand while he thumped the horn with the other. 'We gotta get outta here though,' he muttered restlessly.

But the traffic showed no sign of moving at all.

Barely a minute after Allen had driven off, Dr Ronald Ross had driven his two visitors up to the Museum and had parked in the vacated space. With pompous ceremony he ushered them into the venerable building and led them down to the Research Department in the basement.

Lieutenant Ingram put down his telephone and greeted them grimly. 'Good afternoon, Dr Ross. No doubt you've heard...'

'This is Dr Johanssen and Dr Jarred from the Swedish Institute,' Ross interrupted imperiously.

Ingram stared blankly at the two tall, depressed-looking men in crumpled suits who were looming in the background with jet-lagged expressions. 'But I don't understand, sir,' he mumbled confidentially. 'Dr Kornbluth just left with the Swedish gentlemen a few minutes ago. One of them's been . . .'

'Kornbluth!' Ross shrieked.

Ingram attempted to explain, but he found himself talking to thin air. Ross had rushed off down the side-corridor shouting incoherently, with the bewildered Swedes loping after him.

At the door to the laboratory, Buckhalter sprang to attention and then tried to bar the way, babbling garbled warnings about the danger within, but Ross elbowed him out of the way and burst into the cavernous chamber followed by the two dazed Scandinavians. The basement corridors suddenly rang with shouts and blasts on whistles and marines and FBI agents seemed to emerge as if by magic from the dusty bowels of the museum.

When Ingram, Buckhalter and the others burst into the laboratory, they found Ross and the Swedes motionless on the landing, staring at the cheery smiling figure of Freddie Bauer, who was squatting on the gantry above the tank holding a metal rod with a length of cable attached, which he was dangling in the water like a fishing line.

'Hey, you guys, what kinda bait ya supposed ta use for mermaids?' Freddie boomed, flicking cigar ash into the water and taking a hearty swig from his can of Budweiser.

The Swedes looked as if they had walked into a madhouse.

Freddie beckoned them over. 'Come on, boys, the water's lovely,' he roared.

At last Ross found his voice. 'Let's get after them!' he whined, swinging round on Ingram and his troops. 'And arrest that fat maniac on the tank there.'

As Ingram rushed out with Ross, Freddie paddled his bare feet delightedly in the water and raised his beer can to them in defiant salute.

*

Minutes later a convoy of several army trucks trundled out of the garage underneath the museum and swung into the traffic. Overhead, helicopters rattled up and down the avenues and streets while agents peered down through powerful binoculars in search of the fugitives. Gradually the helicopter units narrowed the field down to the area around the jammed intersection. Then the army convoy advanced as far as it could and the armed marines jumped out of the trucks and started to comb through the stationary cars, trucks and buses in the queue behind the BMW.

Suddenly Walter saw them approaching in the distance through the rear window. 'Move, Bauer, they're right behind us!' he yelled.

Spinning the wheel, Allen accelerated up onto the sidewalk and overtook the jammed lines of traffic, swerving into the side-street at the intersection and bumping back onto the roadway once they had passed the blockage there. Then he took a reckless short-cut through a small park and playground area. Kids enjoying themselves on bikes and in ball games scattered as Allen drove the car round the perimeter path, but two old men sitting at a chessboard on a bench did not even look up from their game as the pigeons rose in a dense cloud in front of the wildly revving BMW. A man selling balloons dived for cover and his multicoloured wares rose into the hazy Manhattan sky, lost forever to the thrilled and terrified customers cowering beside their mums and dads among the bushes.

'Is it a movie?' asked one kid as Allen bounced the car into a shallow ornamental pond and out the other side and through the hedge, roaring away up the street on the opposite side of the park.

At that moment one of the army trucks careered into the square and a helicopter descended over the rooftops and hovered over the trees, sending leaves and loose branches spinning to the ground. The children screamed and cheered in a mixture of terror and delight as the army truck crunched through some flowerbeds, smashed down a length of iron railing and roared away up the narrow street in pursuit of its quarry, while the helicopter tipped forward and swooped away after it.

Allen drove like a demon, the parked cars flashing past on either side in dazzling succession in the narrow street. At the next junction he stamped on the accelerator and flew across, just missing a bus and a taxi. A cacophony of screeching tyres and blaring horns erupted at junction after junction as Allen defied the lights and gunned the engine, sending the car in a series of suicidal swerving turns, left and right, one after the other. Glued to the rear window, Walter felt his heart sinking further and further as more and more army trucks and jeeps joined in the desperate chase behind them and the army helicopters cast their doomlike shadows on the roof.

Allen swept the wrong way round a one-way interchange and then shot into a narrow street lined with parked vehicles where there was just room for the width of the car. As they streaked towards a terrifyingly chancy gap between two garbage trucks parked opposite each other, Walter suddenly yelled to Allen to stop.

'Don't be insane . . .' Allen shouted, his eyes narrowing as he judged the clearance.

'Pull up. Stop the car!' Walter insisted. 'I'll slow the bastards down.'

Allen glanced in his mirror. Three or four jeeps and trucks were staying tenaciously on their tail. 'How the hell will ya do that?' he demanded.

'Just do as I say!'

Allen stamped on the break and the BMW slithered to a halt between the garbage trucks.

Walter flung open the door and scrambled out. 'I caused all this and now I'm gonna finish it,' he shouted through the passenger window.

Madison grabbed his ears, pulled his head into the car and planted a sizzling kiss on his astonished lips, giggling as Walter's thick moustache tickled her face.

Walter blinked, grinned and grunted appreciatively. Then

he ducked out and slammed the door. 'Now get the hell outta here,' he ordered. 'Go, go, go, go...'

Allen waved his hand and the car skidded away.

Standing defiantly erect in the middle of the street between the garbage trucks, Dr Walter Kornbluth turned to face the enemy convoy bearing down on him. His left hand was planted provocatively on his hip, supported at the elbow by the bracket. He raised his right hand with palm facing flat towards the rapidly approaching vehicles, like a revolutionary leader posing for a picture.

The convoy showed no sign of obeying him. Walter waved his hand nervously. Still the trucks and jeeps sped down the narrow canyon towards him. Walter waved his hand frantically and yelled at the top of his voice. Still the convoy bore down on him. At the last moment Walter leaped out of the way onto the sidewalk. His impetus carried him over the edge of an open loading bay and he fell into the trap with a smashing of crates and clanking of tins, plummeting into the basement of a shop as the convoy zipped past unheedingly.

There was a prolonged silence and then a painful stirring sound. Then Walter's plaintive groans issued from the open metal flaps in the pavement. 'Oh God, oh God, oh God. What a week I'm having...'

To his horror, Allen saw in the mirror that the army were still behind him. A few hundred yards further on, he threw the BMW into another narrow side-street. Ahead was a perilously small gap where a cab had parked badly with its rear sticking out at an angle from the kerb. Allen shrugged his shoulders and stood on the accelerator pedal.

'Hold on now, sweetheart!' he shouted to Madison as they hurtled through with fractions of an inch to spare.

Behind them, the jeeps and trucks ground to a halt. A black marine sergeant jumped down and screamed at the cabbie who was sitting on his front wing having a quiet smoke.

'Hey, Mac, move that goddam heap outta the way!'

The cabbie looked up resentfully and slowly took the

cigarette out of his mouth. 'I'm here waitin' for a fare,' he drawled, nodding at a dingy video store across the sidewalk.

The sergeant rapped out an order and a dozen young marines jumped out of a truck. With a chorus of yells they picked up one side of the cab and heaved it over onto the pavement. The sergeant saluted the gaping driver who was watching his vehicle rocking to and fro on its side in the gutter, and the squad climbed back aboard the truck which then led the convoy roaring on its way.

'Keep down, baby,' Allen shouted, as he swung off the street underneath the overhead subway tracks and accelerated up a ramp leading to a pair of locked steel gates. The car smashed through the gates as if they were matchwood and landed with a sickening crunch on the dockside, its overheated engine racing madly. Allen and Madison jumped out and ran hand in hand out along the jutting wharf just as one of the helicopters came beating over the steel viaduct carrying the tracks. The fugitives stood at the far end of the jetty, hugging each other tightly and staring into the heaving oily water of the Hudson River. Madison looked comical and frail clad in Freddie's outsize laboratory coat. Her hair streamed out in the stiff breeze and her eyes were shimmering with tears as Allen held her hard against his bare chest.

'I was ready to stay with you for ever . . .' she whispered.

Allen closed his eyes. 'Yes, yes, I know . . . I know . . .' he stammered, fighting the rising lump in his throat. 'But now that they know who you are, they're never going to leave you alone.'

Madison trembled slightly in the cool wind. 'I can't ever come back to you, Allen,' she murmured.

'Oh, I wish . . . I wish I could go with you,' Allen whispered into her hair, stroking her cheeks with the backs of his fingers.

She moved a little away from him, holding his hands in her own. 'But you can,' she told him simply.

Allen frowned and smiled at the same time. 'I can? How can I?'

'It can be done, Allen.'

'But *how*?' Allen asked, gripping her hands as the helicopter hovered nearer.

Madison drew him closer and spoke quickly. 'Remember when you were eight years old, up at Cape Cod, and you fell off the ship?'

Allen nodded, still not understanding.

'Well, you were safe under the water, weren't you?'

Allen looked past her earnest face and down into the murky water, as if trying to relive that far-off dreamlike experience. 'Yes . . . yes I was. At the beginning, when the little girl . . . the girl . . .'

'You were safe Allen. You were with me.'

Allen still stared at the water, struggling to focus the memory. Then his eyes sank into hers. 'You mean . . . you mean that was you?'

The laboratory coat blew open and Allen felt her firm nipples against his chest. 'That *was* you up at Cape Cod!' he cried, picking her up and whirling her round and round. 'This is great. This is just great!' he cried into the wind. 'I can go with you and come back and still see Freddie at Christmas and still . . .'

'No Allen. You can't ever come back.'

He stopped swinging her and set her gently on the concrete again. His face softened in a momentary wistful smile of hope and longing. Then it hardened abruptly into acceptance of the inevitable.

'Madison . . .' he muttered in a broken voice, unable to even begin to explain the conflict inside him.

She clasped him to her. 'Yes, Allen. I know. I understand.'

Under the threshing blades of the hovering helicopter and with the sound of jeeps and trucks lurching onto the dockside, they kissed in brief, passionate oblivion.

'You down there on the dock. Don't move!' rasped a metallic, disembodied voice from a loudhailer in the helicopter.

Eventually they looked up.

'You are under arrest.'

Allen hugged Madison.

'Just let the girl go,' ordered the official voice. 'Step back from the dock. You are under arrest.'

Allen released his hold of her. 'You must go now,' he murmured in a numb, hollow voice.

They glanced round to see marines starting to jump out of the trucks parked on the wharf.

Allen backed away from Madison. 'I love you, Madison,' he called out. 'Go now.'

But she still stood on the jetty, the voluminous white coat flapping around her. Allen ran forward and pushed her gently towards the edge. 'Go. Go now,' he pleaded wretchedly.

Madison flung off the coat and dived into the river, her body making a high arching curve which took Allen's breath away. Seemingly unaware of all the shouting and bustle around him, Allen stood alone, watching the heaving water at the end of the jetty. As Madison broke surface some distance away, the helicopter flew over him and hovered threateningly above her, its rotors whipping the water into an angry froth.

'Leave her alone!' Allen suddenly screamed out as the Marines mustered on the dockside with several inflatable motor boats. 'Just leave her alone now.'

Madison turned in the boiling water and raised her hand in farewell. Allen waved back with frantic, longing arms as she finally disappeared under the grey swell. A few seconds later, her fin flicked briefly into the air for the last time.

More and more security and army personnel were arriving every moment. Allen saw frogmen preparing to jump from a large helicopter as it appeared round the nearby building and the first of the inflatables was being launched from the dockside.

He hesitated as a group of FBI agents advanced along the jetty towards him. Madison's words echoed round and round in his consciousness: 'I can't ever come back to you, Allen . . . You were safe, Allen. You were with me . . . No, Allen. You can't ever come back . . . You were safe, Allen. You were with me . . . I want to stay with you, Allen. You're the reason I came here . . . You're the reason I came here . . . You're the reason I came here...'

The phrase grew louder and louder and more and more persistent the more he tried to resist its hypnotic effect. He glanced round him at the twin towers of the World Trade Centre, at the New Jersey shore and at the Statue of Liberty across the bay. Suddenly he ripped off his laboratory coat and his shoes and taking the biggest breath in his life, he dived into the water. The FBI agents reached the end of the jetty just too late to snatch him.

Allen floundered frantically in the water, desperately trying to keep himself afloat while he attempted to estimate the direction Madison had taken. The water lashed around him as a second helicopter descended above him and two frogmen poised to dive in after him. Then everything went dark as he began to sink inexorably into the murky depths. Panic-stricken, he flailed around him in the gloom, his lungs burning and pounding in time with his hammering heart. Suddenly the memory of his younger self struggling in the sea off Cape Cod burst vividly into his awareness. Unable to hold his breath any longer, he opened his mouth and gulped and breathed in the deadly water.

The two frogmen dived from the helicopter and swam swiftly towards the telltale trail of bubbles he had released.

When strong hands grasped his Allen thought, with the last traces of his consciousness, that the frogmen had found him and he clutched at the hands gratefully. But then he saw a bright shape suspended beside him and soft fronds brushed his face like a caress. Again he opened his mouth and tried to breathe and now he felt warm life-giving lips press against his. The water seemed suddenly to be illuminated as if the sun had emerged from behind a barrier of cloud. He responded to Madison's kiss and gave himself to her restorative embraces.

They kissed and kissed again. Madison smiled reassuringly and Allen smiled back. Madison drew him through the water and then released him. For a moment Allen panicked, but almost at once he discovered that he need not be afraid. He remembered the feeling all that time ago in the bay at Cape Cod. He began to swim easily and swiftly in Madison's glittering wake as her fluorescent tail drove her steadily through the water in slow, graceful strokes. She turned to see his first tentative movements growing rapidly into strong and confident strokes like her own and she smiled at him with a joyful radiance which strengthened him immeasurably.

All at once they were completely surrounded by frogmen. One grabbed at Madison, but she knocked him away easily with a mere flick of her fin. Then Allen felt himself grasped round the neck from behind. Breaking the diver's hold with an upward thrust of his arms, he turned and seized the face mask. Twisting it to and fro, he finally ripped it off and the diver kicked his flippers and rose quickly to the surface in an explosion of bubbles. Meanwhile Madison had torn the masks off two more divers and they rocketed to the surface in torrents of bubbles. Then she swam in a complicated spiralling pattern and stunned several more frogmen with slicing flicks of her fin as they converged on her.

Allen was attacked again. This time he bit his assailant's ankle and the diver withdrew abruptly like the others, retreating to the surface. Allen was rapidly becoming exhausted by this extra demand on his energy and to his relief Madison glided quickly over to him and seized the sleeve of his shirt, drawing him away with her towards the open sea. As they fled, they hit out at another group of frogmen which suddenly attacked from below. Recoiling with severed pipes, dislodged masks and bruised heads the divers were left floundering helplessly as Madison led Allen irresistibly into clearer and clearer water.

Above the surface, helicopters, jeeps and trucks congregated on the crowded dockside while milling personnel helped the battered and exhausted diving squads back into the rubber boats and onto the wharf. Officers and agents vainly scanned the gently heaving swell through binoculars for some time, searching for a glimpse of their prey. But no sign of the mermaid or of Allen Bauer was ever seen again, except for some clothing which was washed up on the New Jersey foreshore a couple of weeks later.

22

When they were safely out of danger, Madison paused by some weed-covered rocks and kissed Allen with caressing, life-giving lips. Then Allen swam free and took off his clothes and Madison watched happily as he swam round and round her with a new sense of freedom and belonging. He swam to her, twining his legs round her tail and they glided and tumbled in the bright water, kissing and embracing and playfully breaking apart and then coming together again, time after time.

Then Madison led him away and they swam for a long time. Schools of fish parted to let them pass and then reunited and followed them for a while. Gradually the water lightened and lightened until it became transparent and sparkling. Allen cavorted and played around Madison, his body vibrant with newfound life and his eyes filled with enchantment.

Eventually they reached a wall of coral. Madison took Allen's hand and led him down and down until they came to a glowing hole in the gleaming barrier. A brilliantly incandescent light streamed through – as if from some form of submarine star. At first, Allen averted his eyes from the unbearable glare, but as they approached he was able to look. He thought he saw an entire city of pearl and light, of fantastic shapes and colours. He stared into the miraculous vision, like a child watching mysteries in the fire.

Madison turned to him, her eyes filled with promise. She pointed the way through.

Allen gazed at her and then turned to the mysterious portal, his memory of the dark suffocating water and the frantic raucous city already fading to a dim and unlamented shadow.

They glided through into the light and a single image of the old world lingered in Allen's mind. The image of a young boy alone in his own dreams, entranced by the play of light on the water and in the background, on the very edge of his consciousness, the distant voice under the awning across the deck . . .

'Here it comes . . . Watch it now . . . Here it comes . . .'

Allen watched. And it came.